INDIAN WHISPERS

A tale of emotional adventures through India

SURINDER SINGH JOLLY

BLAZING EYES PUBLISHING

CONTENTS

To the memory of my late father and mother, Khushbash Singh and Agya Kaur Jolly.

Also dedicated to my late parents-in-law, Bhagwan Singh and Rani Raj Kaur Gulati, who gave me love and my life partner, my loving wife Gursharan.

❦ 1 ❦

WELCOME TO INDIA

Approaching the border gate from opposite sides were soldiers with their high lifting of legs and aggression on their faces. As they faced each other, heavy foot stomping commenced.

People were cheering, dancing and waving Indian flags. They chanted, "Bharat mata ki Jai" (Victory to mother India).

"Pakistan Zindabad" (Long live Pakistan) shouted the people across the border. The atmosphere was jubilant with the beat of drums, and music blasting on the loudspeakers. Hundreds of spectators on both sides were whipped into a frenzy by compere chanting and the singing of patriotic songs.

Wearing colourful headgear, spreading out like peacock feathers, the soldiers were marching on both sides of the border. When the soldiers faced each other, the posturing and gesturing became more aggressive and the louder everyone cheered. Sandip turned to Taj. "Doesn't this remind you of the All Blacks haka ceremonial dance at the Rugby world cup we attended?"

It was June 2017 and this was the Wagah border flag ceremony between India and Pakistan, held daily at sunset.

The brothers Taj, 29, and Sandip, 21, had arrived the previous day from London.

Taj looked at his younger brother, seeing the excitement in his eyes for their first proper exploration of India together. "Don't be deceived by the festive spirit," he murmured. "Ever since the British partitioned India in 1947, there has been intense enmity between these two nuclear-armed countries. Every year, villagers from both sides of the border are killed in the crossfire."

Heavy for his five foot six and in need of thick glasses, Taj worked as a clinical psychologist in a London hospital while Sandip was taking a gap year following his graduation. Their doctor parents had arrived in England from India in the seventies and had worked in NHS hospitals all over the country.

While Taj was neat, tidy and organised, Sandip was carefree and spontaneous. Six-foot tall with a muscular body, grey eyes and fair complexion, Sandip had always been the more confident of the two. There were times when Taj disapproved of his brother's constant partying and drinking at his university.

Sitting at the border, Taj's mind flitted towards the news stories he'd heard of the frequent border firings between India and Pakistan, which felt a world away from the celebrations and jubilation he was seeing today.

They had been on numerous family vacations to visit grandparents in Delhi but now the brothers wanted to truly explore India, the land of their heritage.

In London, the brothers frequently argued about faith and

culture. Taj would tell Sandip, "You are a coconut, a westernised Indian with little knowledge of Hindu faith and culture. You can't even speak Hindi properly. Ignorance is not bliss."

"I am proud to be British but I also respect Indian culture," Sandip would reply.

"No, you don't. I am your elder brother. Indian culture teaches us to respect our elders. Do you?"

Growing up, Taj had been jealous of Sandip as he felt that his younger brother had been born with a silver spoon in his mouth. During his childhood, Taj's parents worked long hours as junior doctors, often working at hospitals in different cities of UK and necessitating a change of school.

Sandip, on the other hand, had enjoyed a more settled and happier childhood, as by then the family was much better off financially.

Taj pictured the on-call hospital pager in his father's shirt pocket on all his childhood birthday photographs. His memories were suddenly interrupted by a deafening sound.

Fireworks.

"Thank God that blast didn't start a nuclear war!" whispered Taj.

The flags of both countries were being lowered. The massive border gate was closing.

People were happy, full of energy, singing patriotic songs.

Sandip looked at his mobile. He had a message from his network operator. "Welcome to Pakistan."

Sandip was still in India. He wondered what would happen if he entered Pakistan accidentally. Only a short fence separated the farms on either side of the border.

The crowds were dispersing. The vendors were still selling

Indian flags and bottled water. Shops selling alcohol were doing brisk business.

A sign outside one said, "English tourists welcome to Indian Punjab. Cheers."

"Imagine," said Taj, "an English tourist coming from Pakistan, seeing chilled beer being sold on the roadside on a hot Indian day. What would he do?"

"Say cheers, of course," replied Sandip.

Their taxi was waiting to take them to the Sikh holy city of Amritsar, 27 km away.

"Welcome to India," breathed Taj.

❧ 2 ❧

SPIRITUAL JOURNEY

The next day, the brothers visited the Sikh holy shrine, the Golden Temple.

Sikhism was founded in Punjab, India, in the 15th Century by Guru Nanak.

More than 500 years ago, Guru Nanak saw a society divided by caste and inequality where women were regarded as inferior. He preached that women were worthy of praise and equal to men. He preached selfless service to all needy people.

The concept of langar was introduced where everyone irrespective of caste, religion, colour, creed, gender or social status could sit on the ground together as equals and eat the same food. This free meal which is always vegetarian is still served in every Sikh place of worship (Gurdwara) worldwide by volunteers.

There was a sign at the temple entrance. "Remove shoes and cover your head." At one of the stalls around the temple complex, the brothers removed their shoes and socks and were each handed a token with a number on it.

Taj could not believe his eyes as he saw the awe-inspiring golden Harmandar Sahib surrounded by a huge pool, whose waters reflected the gurdwara lights. They joined the women wearing colourful clothes, their heads covered, and men wearing bright-coloured turbans or colourful headscarves. There were hundreds of people on the marble walkway; some sitting around the pool, meditating and praying. Over the speakers, hymns were relayed from Harmandir Sahib. These hymns were from the holy book called Guru Granth Sahibji, which Sikhs revere as a living Guru.

They reached the causeway which was to take them into the inner sanctum. It took over an hour to cover the short distance over the pool. While waiting, they could see fish swimming around in the water. When they reached the front of the queue they had to wait again as only a few pilgrims were allowed in at one time. Finally, they were inside in front of the Guru Granth Sahib. On entering the beautifully adorned space, which was decorated from floor to ceiling, they paid their respects by bowing down on the floor. The priest with the musician was singing a hymn about the power of the mind. Suffering with obsessive compulsive disorder, Sandip knew this well.

He washed his hands with soap many times and he could see that his hands were clean, but until his mind told him that the hands were clean, he could not stop washing.

When they came out of the inner sanctum, the brothers sat on the edge of the pool, the Amrit Sarovar.

"Why are some people taking a dip in the water?" asked Sandip.

"This water is believed to have healing properties," replied Taj.

"You know," said Sandip, "I have always had doubts about the existence of God, but today I felt a serene aura when I saw people praying. I felt having a faith is really beautiful. I would like to thank you for bringing me to this magical, spiritual place."

"Let's have langar," said Taj. "It is considered a blessing. For tourists, it is an experience, but for the needy, it may be the only meal of the day served free and with a healthy portion of respect."

So, they visited the largest free kitchen in the world, the massive langar eating halls, where hundreds were sitting on the floor to eat together. Sandip and Taj sat down on the mats and were served rotis (flatbread made from wheat flour), rice, daal (lentils), a vegetable dish and kheer (dessert).

After enjoying the hot meal, Taj made enquiries and was told, "Usually 90% of the staff is made up of volunteers, some only for a few hours while others volunteer every day. Food is served for up to 100,000 people daily, of all religions and faiths.

The brothers visited the kitchen where they learnt that the volunteers washed 300,000 plates, spoons and bowls each day.

Taj was told, "The yearly budget of running the kitchen runs into hundreds of millions rupees. The expenses are managed through donations from all over the world."

Another volunteer said, "I get so much happiness serving the langar. Here, there is no rich or poor, only good souls."

Taj asked Sandip, "Do you know what the Sikh prayer ends with?"

"I don't."

"Sarbat da bhala," replied Taj. "Plea to God for the welfare and prosperity of all mankind."

"You mean everyone in the world?"

"Yes, because Sikhs believe the same one God resides in every person, irrespective of their faith."

"If leaders of the world believed in this, there would be no wars," exclaimed Sandip.

The brothers did not feel like leaving the Golden Temple, but it was getting late at night and they had to travel to Shimla the following morning.

At the shoe stall, they returned the tokens. The man handed them their shoes.

"These are not my shoes," Sandip told him.

The man shrugged. "Your token number matches the number we put in your shoes."

"My shoes were dirty and muddy; these are clean and shining."

The man laughed. "Look at that group of men and women polishing the shoes of worshippers. They do this out of respect and love for the pilgrims and it teaches humility."

Sandip felt embarrassed and quickly thanked the man.

Taj laughed and told Sandip, "I hope you have learnt the meaning of selfless service."

✵ 3 ✵

TRAVEL TO SHIMLA

Shimla is 342km from Amritsar, in the south western ranges of the Himalayas. It attracts lots of English tourists as in 1864, it became the summer capital of British-India rule and much British history remains in Shimla.

At 8am, they walked to the taxi stand and bartered the fare for their journey to Shimla. Driving through the green fields of Punjab, they noticed that everywhere on Indian highways were lavishly decorated trucks. They travelled with a gleeful disregard for traffic lanes, other vehicles and even the fundamental laws of physics, despite being much overloaded.

Sandip loved reading the brightly coloured signs behind different trucks. "Horn please. Go slow, we meet again but if you go fast, you go up alone. Don't keep smiling at me; you will fall in love."

One truck sign simply said, "Overtake me at your peril."

Most of the trucks had the following phrase painted on the back: "Horn OK please."

Taj asked the taxi driver what it meant.

"They want you to sound the horn before overtaking them," replied the driver.

Sandip groaned. "It should say Horn *not* OK please. The drivers pointlessly sound the horn, causing noise pollution."

"In the cities, drivers honk at red lights as if honking will turn the green signal faster," remarked the driver.

Sandip laughed. "Maybe the lights should change according to the loudness of the honking."

"Then all cities would be full of deaf drivers," said Taj.

They were hungry now. Sandip only wanted to eat at clean and hygienic cafes on the highway although Taj liked the cheap eating places on the highways, called Dhabas, where you could have hot delicious aloo parathas, flatbread stuffed with potatoes and spices, with Lassi, a yogurt-based drink. The taxi driver stopped at a lovely Punjabi restaurant with statues of Punjabi folk dancers at the entrance.

Sandip had butter chicken with tandoori naan while Taj had chole, spiced chickpea curry, with bhature (a soft, fluffy fried leavened bread).

Taj found the dishes too spicy but Sandip enjoyed his meal and was pleased as the premises were clean and cold mineral water was available.

The journey took longer as some anti-government protesters were lying on the highway and there was a traffic jam until the police arrived and removed them.

They reached Chandigarh, 120km from Shimla, in the late afternoon. Chandigarh, the capital of Punjab and Haryana, is considered the best planned city in India.

The taxi driver advised an overnight stay, but the brothers wanted to get on. The driver agreed, provided he got frequent breaks on the way to Shimla on the journey through tortuous mountain roads. As they approached Shimla, the landscape became more beautiful, from lush green meadows to snow-clad mountains.

They reached their destination, a heritage hotel, built during British rule.

In the lobby, they found themselves amid Victorian architecture. Photos of British socialites mingling at tea parties and gala evenings with Indian aristocracy decorated the walls.

Later, when Sandip was enjoying the complimentary snacks in the balcony of his room, he noticed he had visitors.

"Cute little monkeys!" he murmured. Then: "They have taken the chocolates from my plate. The room key is gone too! These monkeys are fearless."

That evening, the hotel security guard told Sandip to be careful with his wallet and camera. "One tourist lost his passport to a monkey, who emptied his coat pockets."

The following day, the brothers decided to visit a Hindu temple on the hill. They stopped at a shop to buy prasad as an offering to God at the temple. The prasad was vegetarian food prepared with rice, milk and sugar.

The shopkeeper advised, "You need a stick to keep monkeys away."

"This is just a sales trick," Taj told Sandip.

After walking some distance, Taj was surrounded by ten monkeys, with open mouths baring their teeth, and grunting. He felt something in his pocket. It was a monkey's hand. He panicked, the prasad fell to the ground and all the monkeys ran to eat it.

"The shopkeeper was right," he conceded. "We should have bought the stick."

Walking up the hill, they met a tourist who told them that a monkey had snatched his glasses.

"Let's go back," said Taj. "If I lose my glasses, I won't be able to see at all."

Sandip was not happy to turn around. He felt Taj was being cowardly but they had to stick together.

On the way back, Taj asked the shopkeeper, "Do monkeys also harass the locals?"

The man laughed. "Oh yes, they do not differentiate." He advised, "avoid taking selfies or showing your teeth to monkeys, as that seems to irritate them."

⚜

NEXT DAY, THE BROTHERS VISITED MUSEUMS AND PLACES OF historical interest where major historical accords were signed, both in British India and independent India.

When visiting Viceregal Lodge, a majestic building built by the British in 1888, Sandip whispered, "Can you imagine British civil servants sitting in this room, discussing and planning the Partition of India in 1947?"

This had been the official summer residence of the British Viceroy and the seat of power of the British empire for six months every year.

"Hard to believe," said Sandip, "that the British ruled the world every summer from this small hill station called Shimla."

The guide said, "In this very building, at the end of the British empire in 1947 after ruling India for two hundred years, the Indian leaders met the last Viceroy, Lord Louis Mountbatten, to discuss partition. The partition was one of the greatest human disasters. On 15th August 1947, across

India and Pakistan 14 million people were displaced and deaths are estimated from 200,000 to 2 million. The new borders split Punjab and Bengal in two, when Muslim-majority Pakistan, a new country, was created. It resulted in massive migration and communal violence, Hindus and Sikhs fleeing Pakistan and Muslims going in the other direction. The trains were arriving on both sides of the border loaded with corpses, giving rise to more anger and more violence. Thousands of women were abducted and raped. The atmosphere of hostility and suspicion between India and Pakistan has plagued their relationship ever since."

Sandip whispered to Taj, "Should the British have stayed longer and arranged for the police and military to plan security before departing?"

"I wish the tragedy had been averted by any means," replied Taj. "I am sorry to say that I feel ashamed that the British authorities ruling during that period treated Partition in such a casual manner that they created a humanitarian disaster."

Changing topic, the guide said, "I can guess why the British made this magnificent hill station their summer capital. It has British weather and the beauty of the Himalayas. Shimla's summer season begins in March and lasts until June with the average high temperature of 24°C."

On the way back, they took a toy train ride from Shimla to Kalka, now a UNESCO world heritage site with its dramatic views of the hills and surrounding villages.

Built by the British in 1906 to connect Shimla to the rest of the Indian rail system, it had more than 100 tunnels and 864 bridges in the rugged mountains.

The longest tunnel is called the kissing tunnel.

Taj was told about a funny incident in the toy train.

A passenger was aboard the train with his wife. Upon entering the kissing tunnel, he accidentally turned the wrong way. As the train emerged from the complete darkness of the tunnel, his wife caught him kissing another woman. She promised that he would never see the light at the end of the tunnel again!

The toy train finished at Kalka.

From there, they took the train to Delhi.

At Delhi station, Sandip noticed a sign. "Beware of pickpockets!"

On reading it, people would immediately put their hands in their pockets to check.

He asked Taj, "Is that how the pickpockets select their victims?"

Taj narrated a story of an Indian businessman who made a big pouch in his traditional long and loose underwear to hide his cash on the train journey.

In the morning, when he woke up in the train, he felt lighter down below.

In the toilet, he was aghast and confused. The hidden pouch was cut and all the money gone. On checking the trouser, all he found was a hole in his back pocket.

"Was it the work of a pickpocket or a laparoscopic surgeon?!"

🕉 4 🕉

EXPERIENCES WITH A FAITH
HEALER

T aj's back screamed with pain. The doctor prescribed
strong painkillers but the pain persisted.

The brothers were staying in a hotel as their
grandparents were not in Delhi. The hotel receptionist advised
a faith healer. He claimed that his relative, who could not
walk, was treated successfully by a healer called Babaji. Taj
didn't hide his scepticism, but as his pain worsened, he decided
to visit.

Babaji sat in a small village, 150km from Delhi. Taj and
Sandip caught a taxi at 4am. It was a wet, monsoon July. The
journey to the village was not pleasant for Taj, his back
protesting at the bumpy road. When they finally reached the
sleepy village, there were queues of people with some lying on
the floor, some on backseats of cars and some in beds, brought
there by villagers.

Taj was told to write his name in the register and take his
waiting number, which was 125. Number 65 flashed on the

screen. Hot and crowded, the waiting room resembled an open courtyard, surrounded by rooms and toilets. They were told the waiting time would be at least two hours and so the taxi driver took them to a tourist hotel on a hill near the village. On the way, they stopped at a park where they saw peacocks. The peacocks had majestically spread their feathers, displaying their beautiful colours, and were dancing in the monsoon rain. The brothers marvelled at the sight and hurried out of the rain to the hotel where they enjoyed a hot masala tea and vegetarian thali served on a big steel plate with partitions. In the plate was daal, aloo gobi (a cauliflower and potato dish), yogurt, rice, chapatis and spiced onion and cucumber salad. The hotel staff told the brothers that people often stayed in the hotel for three days and visited babaji twice a day, morning and afternoon.

Upon their return to visit the healer, the place was teeming with people, some in agony and most with poor mobility. Taj sat in the front of a courtyard waiting his turn. They called fifteen people at a time, who were told to remove their shoes and socks and sit cross-legged on the floor, in full view of the babaji. Taj was nervous when his turn came. He sat down in front of babaji with his hands behind his back.

Babaji told Taj, "your posture is bad. You have to sit with shoulders pulled forward, and do not use your hands to support your back." He told Taj to do five pushups, which Taj did with difficulty. Taj complained that the pains had worsened.

Babaji gave him a glass of water after putting in a teaspoonful of white powder.

Taj felt his body rising from the ground. He looked down.

His feet were not touching the ground. None of the patients in the courtyard were looking at him.

He thought, why are they not amazed to see me going up in the air? Are they not able to see me?

Then he felt Babaji pulling him towards himself. He was laughing. He said, "Son, You are flying. Your body is as light as a feather. You are cured."

Taj felt a twinge in his back. Babaji was standing next to him and told him to do the exercises twice every day and to improve his posture. Babaji touched his spine at the lower back and neck and also the back of both hands. He gave Taj a packet of the white powder and advised him to take one teaspoon morning and evening, dissolved in water. Babaji advised him to avoid taking painkillers or drinking tea. The only fee Taj paid was Rs100 (approx £1.00) for the powder.

He asked Sandip, "Did you see me flying?"

"Are you crazy?" replied Sandip. "You can hardly walk. I think the Indian heat's getting to you."

Taj was amazed at how babaji treated his patients. He looked to be in his eighties but was full of energy. One of the patients was a severely disabled person who was picked up by two young men, his sons. His legs were bent. Babaji touched his legs and his back and seemed to give him some kind of blessing. He made the disabled person hold a railing. One son was told to hold his waist and the other son pulled the legs down until they touched the floor. He made them do this five times despite the screams and protestation from the disabled man. He advised them to do this five times every day at home. Taj wondered whether this was faith healing or was it physiotherapy using faith to convince the devotees?

After two weeks, Taj could now sleep all night. Taj was not sure if this was due to the faith healer or the hot water bottle he applied to his back every night. Taj wondered about his experience of flying. Had it been an illusion or visual hallucination? Was there an intoxicant in the drink?

5

A BRUSH WITH THE LAW

"Want to know a fun fact," said Taj, "about Delhi roads?"

"Go on."

"If a doctor wanted to induce labour in an overdue pregnancy, he would prescribe an auto-rickshaw ride on Delhi roads!"

Sandip rolled his eyes. "You are joking."

"Of course I'm joking."

"But don't you want to experience the chaos of Delhi roads and visit old Delhi?"

"Okay."

Taj rented a car.

Old Delhi is the most historic part of the metropolis with its origins dating back to the Mughal empire in the 16th century.

As they approached old Delhi, the traffic chaos grew.

Being overtaken from all sides, Sandip held his breath waiting to be hit.

He shouted at Taj, "Drive straight. Too many vehicles. They go wherever there is space. Why the hell did you decide to drive?"

The traffic was getting heavier, the sound of horns was deafening. Taj decided to turn back.

He said, "Driving in old Delhi is not for the fainthearted."

Returning to his hotel, he lost his way and turned into a lane which he thought would lead him to his hotel road. There was an open barrier and a security man was talking to a motorist on the side of the barrier. Taj thought that this was a gated residential area and he simply drove through the open barrier. He soon realised that this was a huge industrial complex. Sandip told Taj to turn left but Taj insisted that driving straight would lead them to their hotel.

Suddenly, in front of their car appeared a black van with flashing lights.

Out jumped six uniformed men with guns.

A brusque voice said, "You, come out with your hands raised."

Sandip looked nervously at Taj.

The brusque voice sounded again, loud and threatening. "I will shoot if you don't obey me. I am the security officer.

He was tall and muscular and his hand was on the trigger.

Hands shaking, Sandip came out and was pushed to the ground by two men. One twisted his arms and the other put his knee on his chest.

"You are hurting me. Please stop," begged Sandip.

"That's what we do to terrorists like you," shouted one of the men.

Sandip was sweating. His hands were trembling and his heart was racing.

Both the brothers were handcuffed, frisked and put in a black van with no windows.

After driving about fifteen minutes, the brothers were led into a small office with an armed guard outside. Standing in front of the white wall, first Sandip's photograph was taken, then Taj's.

Two older men walked in, one uniformed and the other in plain clothes.

The uniformed one said, "I am the security in charge. My colleague is from the intelligence department."

Their handcuffs were removed and the group sat around a table.

"Sir, I want to make a phone call," said Taj.

"No, you are not allowed but if you cooperate with us and answer all our questions honestly, I will reconsider."

"Why did you not stop at the entrance barrier? Did you enter on a spying mission?"

"We are not spies. We are tourists. The barrier was open. We had lost our way and thought this was the way to our hotel." Taj gave them the details of the hotel and his grandfather also.

Placing their mobile phones and the two backpacks from their car on the table, the security officer asked them to unlock their laptops and their phones.

Sandip asked, "Why are we being subjected to this interrogation? Show us legal papers before I give you my permission to search my phone and my laptop."

Taj told Sandip to cooperate as they were innocent, and he reluctantly agreed.

The officers left with their phones, laptops and backpacks.

Returning after three hours, the head of security told them

that he was satisfied that they had made a genuine mistake, but if they had turned the car left or right instead of going straight in the factory complex or taken any photographs, he would have sent them to their headquarters for further interrogation. He returned their phones and belongings and gave back their car keys.

Taj profusely apologised and thanked the chief security officer. They were escorted by the security van to the factory entrance. Taj noticed that the entrance barrier was manned by security men. He realised how stupid he had been driving through the open barrier without checking with security officers.

When the brothers reached the hotel, they told the receptionist what had happened. The reception manager said he already knew about the incident, as police had visited the hotel and taken copies of their passports, which the reception had kept. The manager had told the police that they were genuine tourists. The manager told the brothers that they were lucky. "Unauthorised entry to a high-security industrial complex is a very serious matter."

Back in their room, Sandip got into the bed without speaking to Taj.

"I hope you are not blaming me for today's incident?"

"Whose idea was it to drive a rented car in Delhi? Who drove straight through the security gate?"

"Don't blame me for everything. If I had turned left as you told me, instead of sleeping in our room, we would have been in the interrogation cell."

"Perhaps I should thank you, then?"

"Yes."

Sandip took a deep breath and closed his eyes.

For about two hours, Taj could hear Sandip tossing and turning in his bed.

Finally, he said, "Sandip, I'm sorry. I also cannot sleep. I have never been so frightened and humiliated in my life. I know you are also suffering from the incident today."

After a disturbed sleep, Sandip decided to cancel that day's visit to the historical red fort of Delhi.

Taj convinced him that returning to London would be self-defeating, the end of their mission to explore India, though he agreed to leave Delhi for Bhopal.

Taj had a friend in Bhopal, whom he met in London when he was a student there.

Bhopal, a city in central India, is famous for its beautiful lakes.

The overnight train tickets were booked for next day.

❦ 6 ❧

JOURNEY TO BHOPAL

Sandip and Taj arrived at New Delhi railway station. It was a hot sweaty day. The flies were everywhere and even the stray dogs were restless. There was a railway porter haggling with an elderly passenger.

"These are large suitcases to carry. I'll charge Rs500."

"People earn Rs500 for working a full day!"

The coolie picked up the suitcases to assess their weight. "Perhaps they are filled with stones?"

"Come on, be reasonable," the elderly passenger replied. "You are not carrying the luggage on your head anymore as the railway has provided you with a trolley."

"My charges are reasonable."

"OK, my son will carry the bags."

"Wait, pay me Rs350."

"No, Rs250 is reasonable"

"OK, Rs300."

"Agreed."

She followed the coolie over the footbridge to reach

platform number 4. She had to hurry to catch up. The brothers were also travelling from platform 4. People bustled around, and yet despite the noise, some travellers slept soundly on the platform, guarding their bags with their bodies.

Sandip jumped at a sudden loudspeaker blast. "The train to Bhopal is arriving in five minutes on platform 4."

Sandip saw the train before he heard it, astonished by the sight of people hanging out of the carriages ready to jump off as soon as the train slowed to a crawl.

As the train pulled in, the brothers fought their way through the crowds to find the sleeper compartment with their names and the berth numbers on the list outside.

The train started and Delhi's old areas and slums began to float past.

Passengers began to chat to each other and share stories of their travels. The couple in the next berth opened their tiffin boxes and offered potato parathas with chutney to the brothers. Sandip was reluctant but Taj told him, "In India, food is a code of love and you can't say no to people." The brothers joined in and enjoyed the food. A few berths down, a drumbeat started up as a groom to be and his party began a chorus of traditional Indian wedding songs, inviting the rest of the carriage to join in.

As the evening went on and the brothers became more acquainted with their fellow travellers, Taj slipped off to use the toilet. The sign outside the English toilet said, "Not in use."

He used the Indian toilet instead and squatted on the toilet floor. The train was moving fast and the sensation of moving repeatedly sideways left and right helped his constipation but brought on the back pains. With much difficulty, he washed his bottom with water from the lota which was chained to the tap.

The train stopped. He could hear "chai chai" from the tea seller and "Garam anda, garam anda!" from the station vendor selling hot boiled eggs.

There was a notice in the toilet. "Do not use the toilet when the train stops at the station." Taj tried to get up but couldn't because of his back pains.

He looked below and he could see the railway tracks through the big hole of the Indian toilet. He thought, "If I fall down there, no one would know where I had disappeared."

He began to panic.

"Help! Help!" he shouted.

"What is it?" asked a voice from outside.

"Please tell my brother, Sandip in berth 17, that I am locked inside the toilet as I cannot get up!"

Sandip arrived and shook the toilet door hard several times so that the inside lever became dislodged and the door opened.

Taj was relieved.

He told Sandip, "Hold my hands and pull me up."

Sandip looked at the tap next to the toilet floor seat and asked, "Have you used it?"

"Yes."

"Your hands are dirty. I'm not touching them."

"Don't be selfish," shouted Taj.

Sandip held his upper arms and lifted him.

Outside the toilet, Sandip washed his hands many times.

"Why wash so many times? You haven't even used the toilet."

"When I looked at the toilet hole, I was disgusted to see

that you discharged your waste on the rail tracks," replied Sandip.

"With your OCD, how would you ever use the Indian-style toilet?" asked Taj, and then he walked slowly back to his seat.

"I hope the train reaches Bhopal in time tomorrow as I don't want to use the toilet again!" said Taj in agony.

Taj couldn't sleep. He could see passenger suitcases chained with locks to the lower berths. The man on the next berth was snoring loudly. Under his head, his bag was being used as a pillow.

All night, Taj twisted and turned on the hard berth, trying in vain to find a position which would relieve his back pain.

Next morning, the train passed through small villages and green fields. At one station, a man from the compartment got down to drink water from the tap on the platform. The train moved and the station began to float past.

"The train is leaving, hurry up, hurry up," shouted the passengers.

The man ran quickly. There were so many outstretched hands from the compartment to help him. It was Indian comradeship. Luckily, he just made it back in time.

Sandip asked him, "What if a child was left at the station in such circumstances?!"

"Do you know how many children are lost on Indian railways?" replied the man.

"What happens to them?" Sandip asked.

"Many get into the hands of gangs in the sex trade."

There was silence in the compartment, broken only by the announcer's voice. "The train is now approaching Bhopal station."

❧ 7 ❧

POISON CLOUD

Taj's friend Pavan was at the Bhopal station to greet them.

On the way home, he pointed to a building in the distance, behind a vast slum area. He said, "This is the remains of the infamous American pesticide factory. It was built for a bright future in Bhopal but in 1984, all hell was let loose."

"What happened in 1984?"

"There was a chemical leak. This massive slum area was adjacent to the factory. My elder sister's neighbourhood was in the path of the escaping gas. Fortunately, she survived."

Taj wanted to know more so he visited Pavan's sister, Mrs Singh, at home the next day.

She showed him newspapers from that date, some featuring her name.

Taj read the story:

People fled in all directions. Some fell as they stumbled over corpses. They struggled to breathe. Birds were falling from the sky en masse.

Dogs, buffaloes and cows lay dying. Bats were hanging from the branches, dead. Mothers begged drivers of passing cars and trucks to take their children to safety. It was just after midnight on the 2nd of December 1984.

The world's worst industrial disaster was unfolding in the city of lakes, Bhopal.

Mrs Singh had been sleeping in her home near the main Hamidia Road. She was woken by the noise and commotion from the street and went outside to see what was going on.

"I saw hundreds of people running away. There was a dense white cloud and a nauseating offensive smell in the air. My eyes and throat started burning, I felt choked and breathless. My husband drove me to Hamidia Hospital. On the way, I saw many people collapsing. The road was littered with hundreds of slippers and sandals from those fleeing," she told a news reporter.

When she reached the hospital, she was among thousands of people frantically trying to get in. "People were coughing and vomiting blood; they had bloodshot eyes and froth foaming from their mouths. Some had fits and collapsed. I saw little children crying, looking for their mothers," she continued.

Dr Sinha, a junior doctor, was working in the Emergency department of the Hamidia Hospital.

She asked her senior doctor, "How do I manage these patients? What can I do?"

The consultant replied, "We are struggling to get any detailed information. We don't even know the composition of the leaked gas. Keep patients hydrated. Wash their eyes and skin with water. Such gases are known to cause acute heart failure, so oxygen is mandatory for every patient."

Mrs Singh noticed that while putting the needle in her arm vein, Dr Sinha was so tired that her eyes were closing and she was shaking her head to keep herself awake but she managed to start the intravenous fluids.

Dr Sinha was barely five feet tall but her courage was immeasurable.

Despite her best efforts, people were dying. She would take a deep breath and move on, to treat the next patient.

Mrs Singh cried as the reporters recorded her story.

She said, "The next day, when I looked out of the window, I could not believe my eyes. There were hundreds of dead bodies in the hospital grounds and people were trying to identify their relatives."

Inside the hospital, doctors and nurses were running all over to help distressed breathless patients.

The wind blew the toxic cloud towards nearby slums, the railway station half a mile away, and to the overpopulated parts of the old city a mile away.

At the railway station, some of the coolies, the porters who hid in the waiting room with the room windows barred and their faces covered with a damp cloth, survived. When they stepped on the platform, it was as if a massive bomb had fallen. Hundreds of dead and dying were lying together in the nightmare of death. Babies died in their mothers' laps sucking their thumbs.

The coolies noticed lots of people had froth coming out of their mouths and their lips and hands were bluish.

They put people who they thought were alive on their trolleys and took them to Hamidia Hospital.

One man's limbs were moving but the doctor said, "He is

actually dead. It seems the gases are causing the muscle spasms even after death."

They put other patients on oxygen and one miraculously made enough of a recovery to speak.

He told the doctor, "When I stepped out of the train, I saw a foggy cloud invading the platform, travelling along the ground. I think I lost consciousness straightway."

The doctor said, "It is amazing that you survived the poison cloud. I wish others had your luck."

In the path of the gas, the only people unaffected next morning were those who slept unaware inside their homes with windows closed in this cold December month.

❧ 8 ❧
WORKERS' DEMONSTRATION IN
BHOPAL 2017

Thousands of people were marching, some beating drums, big Indian drums. There were red flags everywhere.

"Down with exploitation."

"Power to the workers."

"Down with corruption."

"Down with corporate greed."

"Workers of the world unite."

When the leader announced, "We demand justice for the gas victims," people cheered loudly.

On the stage was a man wearing dark glasses.

He said his name was Jatindra.

On the night of 2nd December 1984, he was sleeping when the phone rang.

It was his employee at the petrol station complaining of breathlessness. To help him, he left his home quickly.

On the way on his motorbike, he felt a stinging sensation in his eyes.

As his vision was getting blurry and painful, he stopped his bike.

Hundreds of people were coming from the opposite direction. One kind gentleman gave him water to wash his eyes and took him to the hospital. The doctor said the chemicals in the leaking gas had burnt his eyes. Since that day in 1984, he has been blind.

He raised his voice and said, "Hundreds of people suddenly blinded in one night. What was their fault? Because they were unfortunately in the path of the leaking gas. Don't they all deserve an apology? Aren't the people of Bhopal owed an apology? WHERE IS THE APOLOGY?"

People shouted, "Shame, shame."

Taj asked the leader, "Sir, I am from the UK. What justice are you demanding for gas victims?"

"Do you not know what happened on the night of 2nd December 1984?" asked the man in disbelief.

"I know, but please tell me more."

"Half a million people were exposed to methyl isocyanate gas and other chemicals. Over 3000 dead were counted in the first 72 hours. The total deaths related to gas exposure to this day, has exceeded 10,000. It has now been more than three decades since the industrial disaster. The chemical company paid us inadequate compensation. The chemical waste was left behind at the factory site. Our beautiful city of lakes has been scarred forever."

He went on, "Babies born to mothers who were exposed to the leaked gas had genetic defects. Cancer cases have risen in Bhopal. Who will compensate for gas-related new disabilities? Who will compensate the dead and the living dead, who struggle to breathe every day? Our rights as poor Indians have been trampled upon."

He introduced Taj to a survivor, an old man who said, "I was one of the thousands of people who lived in the slums next to the factory wall. I still have nightmares of little children gasping for breath and dying."

As the march wound through the narrow streets of old Bhopal, a man threw a firecracker at the police. He was arrested and as the police led him away, some demonstrators started throwing stones. There was teargas and panic as people fled the scene.

The leader looked at the street littered with stones and said, "What a waste. A small minority spoiled our completely peaceful protest. We should be standing with poor gas victims, not fighting with our police."

EVENTFUL WEDDING

Over dinner, Mrs Singh told Taj about an eventful wedding in Bhopal.

Wedding guests panicked and ran off as quickly as they could. There were frantic voices coming from outside. "Bhago, run, gas leak."

Four hours ago, the bridegroom had ridden up to the entrance gate of the wedding venue on a white horse with his little nephew sitting in front of him.

He was wearing a headdress of garlands of beads called sehra, covering his face.

The drummers preceded him. Behind him, the people in the groom's party were dancing with the band playing Bollywood music. Everyone was happy. It was the wedding of Dalip to Aditi.

Dalip wore a white silk sherwani – a long coat-like jacket up to the knees – and a turban with a silk brocade on the exterior with elaborate broaches all around. He had a golden dupatta (scarf) and red-embroidered sherwani shoes.

The bride's parents welcomed the bridegroom and his family. After the welcome ceremony, the guests were led to the venue grounds.

The wedding venue was a grand hall with massive gardens. The entrance gate was decorated with an arch of fresh flowers, full of red, white and yellow roses. It was surrounded by hundreds of strings of multi-coloured lights.

The trees were decorated with drop lights. There were floating candles (diyas), marigold flowers and rose petals in the pond, at the corner of the garden.

In the middle of the garden, there was a small platform, decorated with more white flowers and open to the auspicious stars. Here, the priest sat around the small fire that would be the witness of their religious vows.

Aditi arrived, with her friends and extended family.

She wore a pink sari with pink bindi on her forehead. Her silk sari had rich golden embroidery with glittering stones. She was adorned with gold jewellery. All the ladies wore a lot of jewellery and their hands and feet were covered with henna patterns. The children, dressed in their best clothes, were running around. It was a happy atmosphere.

Dalip placed a garland of red, heavily fragrant roses around her neck.

As she took her turn in garlanding Dalip, her gaze remained low, remembering her mother's instructions to avoid eye contact in public.

One of the foreign guests shouted, "Come on, kiss each other."

Some elders looked at him in anger.

One said, "This is India. Here, no kissing in front of other people. Please respect the Indian culture."

The guests milled and chattered around the lawns. They coalesced into little groups, the men here, the women there, around the heaters placed strategically around the garden. They were gossiping about other people's children, while their own children were flirting in the main hall. Scandals and rumours in the community were discussed with lots of laughter and head shaking.

The photographer was busy clicking.

He told the guests, "Say cheese, everyone."

With their mouths full of cheese pakoras, they put on their biggest smiles.

There was the scent of flowers, perfumes and cooked spices.

A man asked his young son, "What's mum doing?"

"Exactly the same as you, laughing at other people's problems. Dad, let's go and eat in the main hall."

"OK, you find out where they are frying the sweet jalebi and we will go."

"First, you come with me to the ice-cream stall," replied the son.

There were at least twenty five stalls all around the garden and in the main hall serving food and drinks, all paid for by the bride's parents. The guests were enjoying Punjabi, Rajasthani, Gujarati and many South Indian delicacies along with Chinese food and pizzas, all flavoured with Indian spices. The waiters brought snacks, fruit juice, tea and coffee to people standing in the garden.

It was an arranged Hindu marriage. As was the custom, three months ago an astrologer had decided the date of marriage.

The astrologer said, "Matching of stars as per the

horoscope of the boy and the girl is essential for the marriage. Your fate is decided by three things in life. Your date of birth, your place of birth and most importantly your time of birth."

He studied the horoscopes of Dalip and Aditi and decided the date and time of their marriage.

Date: 2nd December 1984.

Time: Between 11PM and 1 AM.

The astrologer advised, "Marriage is not only the union of boy and girl but of both families also. The stars on that date are favourable for compatibility of both the couple and their families."

Dalip timidly asked, "Do the stars favour love in our marriage?"

"Love always comes after marriage, like monsoon follows the hot summers," replied the astrologer.

Clad in a sari, Aditi was feeling cold on this chilly December night. Standing near an outdoor heater in the garden, she looked at the time. It was exactly eleven o'clock.

The announcement came over on the loudspeaker. "The wedding rites are going to start soon. Please join us for your blessings."

The father of the bride placed his daughter's hands in the groom's. The priest offered crushed sandalwood, ghee, herbs and rice to the fire while reciting Vedic prayers.

The couple walked around the fire while taking solemn vows of loyalty and lifelong fidelity to each other amidst the chanting of sacred mantras.

The bride and groom repeated the prayers spoken by the priest. The couple had to circle the sacred fire seven times to complete the wedding.

The 5th phera (Hindu religious rounds around the holy fire) of the marriage were completed and two pheras were left. The screaming from outside was getting louder and louder. Dalip could not ignore the commotion and most of the guests and the photographer were leaving. He looked at his father who took over the stage and announced, "We are stopping the pheras and god willing, we will complete them tomorrow. I have contacted the police. There is gas leaking from the chemical factory. Please do not go towards the railway station or the old part of Bhopal city. The new Bhopal area seems to be safe. May God protect you all."

The next day, both families made the decision to complete the wedding in a different venue, much away from the gas-stricken areas. The last two pheras around the sacred fire with the priest chanting holy mantras were completed.

The groom then applied the sindoor, a red powder, to the parting in his bride's hair.

He also put the mangal sutra around her neck. This necklace, made up of gold and black beads, was meant to be worn always by the bride as a symbol of her marriage, along with the sindoor in her hair.

The couple touched the feet of both their parents and were blessed by them.

Dalip and Aditi could at last smile for the photographer, relieved that the religious ceremony had been completed and they were now husband and wife.

The guests queued to give their gifts and have their photograph taken with the couple. Aditi noticed there were far fewer guests. She worried about the ones who failed to attend, hoping that they are all safe.

At last, it was time to go to her husband's home. The

chauffeur-driven Mercedes arrived, decorated with strings of flowers.

With tears running down her cheeks, Aditi hugged her mother.

The mother said, "My darling daughter is leaving us to start a new life. I am happy for you but also heartbroken today." She sobbed and smiled simultaneously.

Aditi's eyes were red and her nose and cheeks were flushed with weeping.

Someone shouted, "The bride cries for one day on her wedding day; the groom cries for the rest of his life!"

Aditi also hugged her father, who helped her into the car.

As the car started, the father threw coins in front of the car as per the tradition. The street children ran to collect the coins on the road.

Dalip gave her a tissue to wipe her eyes.

He said, "What an eventful wedding. Thank God we are all alive."

Aditi said, "When people congratulate us, I think of the suffering in our city and feel sad. Our beautiful city is traumatised. I was thinking of giving our cash gifts towards helping the families who have lost their breadwinners."

"I agree. It is a noble idea."

She held his hand. "I love you."

WHERE'S MY CHILD? BHOPAL SAGA CONTINUES

T aj visited a charity dealing with the missing children of Bhopal. This is the incredible story narrated to him by one of their volunteers.

ॐ

CRYING ON THE ROADSIDE, WAS A YOUNG WOMAN.

"I cannot find my son. I was holding his hand and then I got pushed by the crowds. I fell down and when I got up, my child was not there. I looked everywhere but could not find him. Please help me," she sobbed. "He is only two years old."

An elderly man told her, "If you stay here, the gas leak will kill you. Go to Hamidia hospital. You may find your child there."

When she reached the hospital, there were many crying children looking for their parents. Her son was nowhere to be seen. She knelt down and sobbed uncontrollably. "It is all my fault. I should not have let go of his hand."

A nurse consoled her, helped her to get up and asked, "What is your name?"

"My name is Mamta. I live in the slums adjacent to the American factory. We were fleeing the gas leak when I lost my child. I am a poor building labourer. All I had in my life was my son, Arvind."

"Don't worry," reassured the nurse. "We will look in every hospital ward. We will find your child."

But the search was in vain.

Mamta heard that mass cremations for Hindus and burials for Muslims were taking place. She rushed to both sites and showed her son's photograph everywhere, but drew a blank and all she received were sympathies.

As weeks turned into months, she started losing hope of finding her son alive. Every morning, she would visit the local Hindu temple and pray, "God, please make a miracle. Give me my Arvind."

Mamta was tall and thin with a dark complexion. She had long black hair which she tied in a simple ponytail. Her hands were rough and her face showed scars of fallen bricks from the years of balancing them on her head, while climbing stairs on the building site. Her husband, a gambler, would beat her when she accused him of stealing her money. One day, he walked out of her life and never returned.

One evening, she was walking through New Market shopping area of Bhopal, when she caught sight of a child's photograph in the window of a photo studio. Her heart skipped a beat as she ran over to take a closer look. It was a birthday photograph of a child blowing a candle.

Her eyes widened when she read the inscription on the cake, "HAPPY 5TH BIRTHDAY ARVIND."

She rubbed her eyes. "Am I dreaming? My Arvind would have been five years old this month. But this child is wearing smart clothes with a bow tie and expensive polished shoes. How could he be my Arvind?"

She asked the shop attendant about the photo. He said the photographer, the shop owner, was out on a job and would not return that day. He would be available the following day at 9am.

Reluctantly, she left the studio, glancing back again and again at the birthday photograph.

That night, she could not sleep. Her mind repeatedly wandered to the birthday photograph. "Is he my Arvind or just a resemblance? Is his birthday in January just a coincidence? Please God, help me. I am confused."

At 6am the next morning, she reached the temple. She rang the bells and prayed for Arvind.

Then she started walking towards the New Market studio. With each step, her heart raced. She reached the place at 7am, two hours before the opening of the shop.

On the pavement next to the paan shop, she sat down. She noticed red paan stains matching her red sari all over the pavement.

As the clock ticked on, she began to shiver in the cold January morning. Her hands and feet were slowly becoming numb, and yet she barely noticed as she lost herself in thoughts of Arvind. Only when she saw a group of people huddled around a small fire did she become aware of her own plight, so she got up and joined them. They were a family of manual labourers who had migrated from their village in search of employment in Bhopal. No one spoke and the only movement came from the labourers adding further scraps of wood to the fire by the side of the pavement. A barefoot child of Arvind's age watched Mamta as she stared into the fire. His mother put a blanket on him to keep him warm as he cuddled into her.

Mamta returned to the pavement outside the studio with a cup of tea. The shop owner arrived at nine o'clock and opened the studio. Mamta walked in, pointing towards the birthday photograph. "Please, I want to meet this child. I am Arvind's mother."

The shop owner looked at her, a woman wearing an old sari with worn-out chappals and holding an empty plastic cup. "What nonsense. How could a beggar be the mother of a rich boy? Get out of my shop."

Tears welled in her eyes. She walked out and sat on the pavement opposite the studio. She was now shivering with anxiety, confused at what to do next. It started raining and she got all wet but she kept watch, hoping that Arvind would visit the studio.

Some hours later, the sun came out, slowly bringing warmth. A big car suddenly arrived. The driver opened the rear door and out came an older couple with a young boy.

When Mamta realised that the boy was her Arvind, she rushed towards them shouting, "My Arvind, my baby." He hid behind the man. The man stopped her and asked, "Who are you?"

"I am Mamta. I lost my son, Arvind, on the day of the Bhopal gas disaster near the slums adjacent to the American factory. I have his photograph." She emptied her bag and an old photograph of Arvind fell from her trembling hands. The man picked it up. He asked Mamta to come inside the shop.

Mamta folded her hands and said, "Sir, please, can I have my Arvind back. I have shown his photograph."

The man replied, "That does not prove you are the mother. Tell me any distinguishing features. Do you have any documents and his birth certificate?"

"I do not have any documents, but I had his name ARVIND tattooed on his right forearm when he was a baby."

The man asked, "any other distinguishing features?"

"Yes, when he was born, he had a bruise on his low back. Then, it became a permanent bruise. People thought that I was beating him but it was like a birthmark."

Convinced that Mamta was telling the truth, he explained, "I am Mr Banerjee. I am a rich businessman. On the day of the gas leak, me and my wife were travelling near the slums. Our driver braked hard when he saw a child standing on the road. Thousands of people were fleeing. We realised that this child was lost. My wife hugged the child and said, 'God has sent this baby for us.' We were childless, so we gave all our love to Arvind. We brought him up like a prince."

Mamta said, "In the last three years, there is not a night I have not cried for Arvind. I am a poor labourer and I have no one except him."

"That is precisely why I want to help you," said Mr Banerjee. "We would give him the best education. He would become a rich man if you leave him with us. I will give you enough money to lead a very comfortable life."

Mamta started crying. "Please don't take my child away in the name of money. My life has been hell without him."

Mr Banerjee looked nervously at his wife, who was sweating with fear and whose hands were shaking.

Mrs Banerjee spoke in a trembling voice. "Arvind has given

us so much happiness in the last three years. Why can't he have two mothers and you can stay with him in our house."

"Could I stay close to my baby?" asked Mamta.

"Yes," replied Mrs Banerjee.

Mamta looked at her. In her fifties, she was about five feet and wearing an expensive silk sari and lots of gold jewellery. Standing next to her was Arvind, who had been listening to their conversation.

Mamta knelt on the ground beside Arvind.

He moved further away, saying, "You are not my mother."

Tears rolled down her cheeks. "I yearn to hold him in my arms. I have waited for three long years."

Mrs Banerjee said, "Don't worry, when you spend time with him, he will start loving you."

"Okay, I will stay with him in your house," said Mamta.

Heaving a sigh of relief, Mrs Banerjee hugged her.

The photographer looked at them in amazement.

Mrs Banerjee told her, "Call me didi (sister). Let's go home."

They all sat in the car. Mamta felt strange. She had never seen the inside of a car and this was a big posh car. When they entered the long driveway of a house looking like a palace, Mrs Banerjee turned to Mamta and said, "Welcome to our house."

Two small dogs came running from the big garden and jumped around Arvind. Mamta saw the happiness on his face.

Next to Arvind's bedroom, a room was given to Mamta. She was shown around the huge house. Arvind's toy room was bigger than their entire hut in the slums. His nanny also had her own room. Mamta was surprised to learn that there were ten live-in servants. It seemed they inhabited another planet.

Despite spending lots of time with Arvind, he treated her no different than his nanny.

Some nights, Mamta would cry and ask God, "You have given me my Arvind back but he has no love for me."

One day, Mamta asked Mr and Mrs Banerjee, "Could I please show Arvind the building site, where I worked?"

They agreed but wanted her to go in the car with their driver.

Her co-workers at the building site came running to meet her. They knew Arvind as he would play with their children on the pile of sand next to the cement mixer.

Mamta's mind wandered to her old days. She would take breaks to breastfeed Arvind on the hot summer days, when the temperature would be more than 40 degrees Celsius. There would be dust storms and she would run to cover him with a thin cloth. She would put him on a sack of cement under the shade of a tree with a plastic bottle of water. She would make a swing by tying a sheet of cloth to the wooden bar and push the swing when he cried, while shifting bricks on her head. When he was one and a half years old, she got a shock of her life. He crawled up the half-built stairs and fell from the first floor – luckily onto a big pile of sand.

Now, Arvind looked at the women working at the building site with curiosity. They would put a roll of cloth on their heads. Over that, a wooden plank and twelve bricks. The women wore brightly coloured low-waisted saris and a choli/blouse with shiny jewellery at the neck, waistline and ankles.

Arvind looked at the children playing in the sand and on the cement sacks.

He thought, *Why are they not wearing shoes? Their faces and hairs are covered with sand. Why does no one tell them to stop playing in the dirt?*

It was a hot afternoon. The women invited Mamta and Arvind to their lunch. They sat under a banyan tree and ate their chapatis with salt and onions. Arvind refused to eat. He made faces and shrugged his shoulders.

It was time to go home. The women wanted to kiss him on the cheeks but he quickly got into the car. "No, don't come near me, your clothes are dirty."

Mamta thought, *Is he the same Arvind, who was looked after by these women, who ate this poor lunch daily and played with these poor children?*

It was four months since Arvind came back in her life. Later that day, while playing snakes and ladders, he looked at Mamta and for the first time ever, called her, "Mom."

She hugged him tightly and with tears in her eyes, she prayed, "Thank you God for giving me back my baby. Unite all the children and parents separated in the gas disaster. Please end the suffering of the people of Bhopal."

BHOPAL LAKE

Sandip and Taj hired a pedal boat and pedalled around the small island in the middle of Bhopal lake. There is a myth that when this small island is covered by the lake water, the city of Bhopal shall also drown.

Crossing colourful sailing boats, they saw a bigger boat called 'Cruise on the lake', full of people eating and dancing to loud Bollywood music.

"Have you noticed," said Taj, "how the Indians love their Bollywood and food. Even a public park here has vendors selling snacks and frying Indian sweets. Imagine a UK public park, with vendors selling fried food."

It was a windy day and the white clouds were moving fast, as if there was a race in the sky. The lake was getting crowded with speedboats trying to race each other.

The sky was now bright orange and red, illuminating a quivering path across the water. It was time to return the pedal boat.

Feeling hungry, they walked to the Wind and Waves

restaurant on the hillside next to the lake. They had masala tea and Dosas, a south Indian delicacy. It was getting dark but the ribbons of flickering moonlight on the lake water as the clouds moved past the moon was magical.

The brothers visited the lake again in the early morning. The trees on the hill on the other side of the lake were shrouded in the mist. Thin white clouds flew low over the water as if they had just risen from the lake. A bird dived into the water to catch fish. A white boat was anchored on the shore, still in this beautiful calm of nature. The fisherman was focusing on his catch. The dark and the white clouds seemed to be fighting for space in the sky. The sun rays coming through the black clouds made a web of amazing beauty. The lake glistened in the sun like pearls and diamonds. Taj felt that the calm waters and the moving clouds had the effect of mindfulness on him.

While walking along the lake, they came across a group of people sitting crosslegged with eyes closed, doing breathing exercises. Taj joined them, but struggled to sit in the same manner.

"Sorry, I suffer with back pains," he explained.

"Then it is even more important for you to do yoga to strengthen your core muscles. Come to the lake every morning. We will teach you the exercises," said the yoga teacher.

"How will breathing exercises help?"

"Learning to control breathing leads to good health. Do you know why a sadhu meditating in the path of the Bhopal gas leak survived while people around him were dying?" asked the yoga teacher.

"No," conceded Taj.

"He controlled his breathing to stop inhaling the toxic gas."

"Incredible India," said Sandip.

Next morning, the brothers were taken by their friend Pavan to an open park. There were lots of people sharing the space on the morning of this hot summer day. Some were walking fast, a few were jogging and many were exercising in the open gym. Taj complimented an elderly couple who were enjoying exercising together.

They replied, "We come daily, it is a free open gym, all the equipment is weather resistant and does not need electricity to operate."

Then, they came across a group of people laughing loudly. Taj enquired and was told that they were practising Laughter Yoga.

With their arms raised in the air, standing in a circle were about ten people, mainly middle-aged men but a few women also.

The gentleman leading the group was saying, "Take a long breath in through your nose and slowly breathe out through your mouth. Stretch your arms out as if you are going to fly, now laugh loudly, more loudly, now say *very good, very good* and clap your hands."

"How does it help you?" Taj asked the group leader.

"Forced laughter soon turns into real and contagious laughter. It can help beat stress, anxiety and depression. We meet every morning at this end of the park to begin our day with laughter. Why don't you join us?"

Sandip told Taj, "It could help you in London also. The next time you spot a traffic warden putting a parking ticket on your car, do laughter yoga. It is contagious and perhaps he will also laugh and cancel your parking fine!"

"If he doesn't double it," replied Taj with a chuckle.

The brothers noticed another group. They were senior citizens discussing politics. The only difference with *Question Time* on the BBC, was here they shouted at each other with so much passion, you could not hear what anyone was saying.

"India is noisy, we have to shout to get the message through!" quipped one of the gentlemen when asked why they were shouting.

Next, they had fresh coconut water from a stall.

In the car on the way back, Sandip looked back and screamed, "Speed up Pavan, lots of stray dogs are chasing the car."

When they reached home, Sandip was nervous opening the car door.

Taj told Sandip, "Don't panic. Do laughter yoga and maybe the stray dogs will join the laughter!"

SANDIP CRIES

That night, Sandip awoke to the sound of retching from the bathroom. Taj was vomiting.

Next day, Pavan noticed that Taj's eyes were yellowish.

He took him to his family doctor. The doctor diagnosed acute infectious hepatitis, which he explained is usually caused by drinking contaminated water.

He continued, "There is no specific treatment for this viral condition. It usually improves without any medication."

Over next few days, Taj suffered with recurrent vomiting. He could not eat or drink.

Pavan took him back to his doctor. This time, the doctor admitted him to the local hospital.

Blood tests revealed that Taj had jaundice.

"You are so dehydrated that I am struggling to find a good vein to insert the needle in, but you desperately need intravenous fluids." The white-coated junior doctor was bending over Taj, trying to feel a vein on his hands and forearms, after two failed attempts. When Taj saw the relieved smile on the young doctor's face, he knew the vein had been found and intravenous fluids had started.

Despite this, he still suffered vomiting and abdomen pains.

Daily blood tests in the hospital revealed that Taj's jaundice was progressively getting worse. His eyes, skin and urine were very yellow.

Sandip was worried and visited the Hindu temple Birla Mandir, on the top of Arera hills, to pray for Taj's health. Sitting outside the temple, he could see the Bhopal city lights below and the lake in the distance. His mind wandered to his brother's health and tears welled up in his eyes. He had a frightening thought of losing his brother. He had looked up to his older brother for advice and confided in him, knowing he would keep it all a secret from their parents. He remembered when he was bullied by two boys in his school and told to go back to his country after being kicked in the corridor. Then, he was frightened of going to school or telling his parents, but Taj protected him.

The next day, Sandip arranged a meeting with his brother's consultant, who advised transfer to a specialist liver unit in Delhi.

Sandip booked a flight. He also informed his parents in London.

In the liver ward in Delhi, Taj was put again on intravenous fluids.

The consultant advised a liver biopsy.

Taj asked if it would cure his jaundice.

"No, it will not cure you, but it would help us to understand your liver disease and improve our management of your condition."

Next day, Sandip noticed Taj was staring blankly into the space. Then suddenly, all his limbs were shaking violently. Sandip shouted for the nurse. Taj's fit suddenly stopped. He seemed drowsy.

The doctor checked him and told Sandip, "Don't worry. I'm doing blood tests."

Taj slept for about three hours and when he awoke he asked Sandip, "Are we travelling in a train from Birmingham to London?"

"No, you are in a hospital in Delhi."

"Why is the ticket collector here?" asked Taj.

"Where?"

He pointed towards the doctor in the white coat.

Sandip told the doctor about the conversation.

The doctor said, "After a fit, patients are sometimes confused. I am also checking for liver failure."

Sandip asked with a worried look, "You mean, his liver could have failed completely?"

"His jaundice was so severe. It signifies that there was substantial damage to his liver," replied the doctor.

At that moment, his parents, who had flown from London, entered the ward.

Sandip wept and hugged them. He updated them on Taj's condition.

His grandfather was also with them.

He said, "I know a herbal practitioner, who has a remedy for all liver diseases."

Their father said, "Taj is suffering with severe liver problems and you want to experiment with questionable herbal products?"

"Yes, yes, because we want our Taj to be cured."

"I won't let you play with my son's life."

"Do you have a cure for severe liver damage in your allopathic medicine?" asked the grandfather.

"No, but they are doing the liver biopsy to investigate further. Don't forget, I am a doctor," said Dr Kohli.

"Do you think I would ever do anything to harm my grandson?" Tears welled up in his eyes.

Dr Kohli gave in.

He told his father, "We need your blessings, not your tears."

They telephoned the herbal practitioner in Kerala, South India.

He agreed to come to Delhi. His airline tickets and hotel accommodation were arranged.

Next day, he arrived and visited the hospital.

An elderly man, he wore thick glasses and had a white bushy beard. He wore a white shirt and black trousers.

Sitting next to Taj on his hospital bed, he asked, "Do you drink alcohol?"

"No."

He looked at his yellow eyes and asked, "What is the colour of your urine?"

"Dark yellow."

"What colour is your stool?"

"Very pale."

He checked his pulse for a long time and said, "English medicines have damaged your liver. The modern allopathic medicines cannot grow damaged liver but in India, we have the herbal preparation which can cure your liver and jaundice problem."

"I'm having a liver biopsy tomorrow."

"No. You cannot have it while taking my treatment."

He gave him a powder to be mixed with water and taken twice a day.

Taj told his consultant that he wanted to defer the liver biopsy but he did not tell him the reason, nor did he tell him that he was taking a herbal remedy.

Taj's father was unhappy about delaying the liver biopsy.

He asked the practitioner, "What has your herbal treatment to do with a liver biopsy?"

"If the biopsy is done, it will interfere with my treatment."

"I am a doctor from London. I don't think it would cause any problems. Taj should proceed with biopsy."

"If it is so, I will stop my treatment. If you don't trust me, there is no point in me treating your son."

Taj's grandfather intervened. "I trust you. Please proceed with your treatment."

The herbal practitioner came every day to the ward and checked Taj's pulse.

His hospital consultant was astonished when the daily liver blood tests showed dramatic improvement. The yellowness of Taj's eyes and skin improved. He started eating and drinking.

When the consultant came for his ward round, he was pleased to see Taj smiling and his eyes and skin were their normal colour. He was surprised on checking the recent blood liver tests. They were normal!

He said, "This is a miracle. I have never seen such a dramatic improvement in ten days in a case of such severe jaundice. I plan to discharge you today."

Taj asked, "Sir, what was the cause of my jaundice?"

"The liver biopsy may have suggested the cause but it does not matter, you are cured now. You can go home."

Taj muttered, "We must thank the herbal doctor. He cured me."

Taj and his father visited him in his hotel to thank him, where Dr Kohli begged the practitioner to tell him the name of the herb which had cured his son. The herbal practitioner refused, but did say that the medicinal plant grows in the foothills of the Himalayas and helps even a severely damaged liver to regenerate.

Dr Kohli paid the herbal specialist handsomely and said, "You have saved my son's life. Are you able to share the details of this miracle herb so that we can open a liver clinic in London? You will be a millionaire. There is so much liver disease due to alcohol in UK."

He replied, "I am able to cure liver diseases because this herb secret was passed to me from my ancestors, and I will pass it on to my son and he will continue to cure people and this will be his livelihood. I also believe the day I sell my herb secret, it will lose its power to cure people. That's why I do not share this secret with anyone."

Dr Kohli sighed, wishing he could change the practitioner's mind but understanding that this man had saved his son's life, and he needed to respect his wishes.

Sandip took the contact details of the herbal practitioner from his grandfather.

He thought, *I now know who to contact if I suffer with alcoholic liver disease. Cheers!*

❧ 13 ❧

WHAT A FLIGHT

Back in good health, Taj spent several days with his grandparents.

Sitting in his grandfather's house, a neighbour narrated his honeymoon story to Taj. He said, "Some forty years ago, I had recently married. I wanted to show off to my wife, so I telephoned the Delhi airfield number to enquire about private flights to Himachal Pradesh, to enjoy the beauty of Himalayas.

"The lady replied, 'Yes, we have a twelve-seater private plane, you come to this private airfield at 8am and when we get twelve passengers, we fly.'

"The airfare was reasonable.

"Excited, I told my wife, 'We are flying tomorrow in a private jet to Kullu to celebrate our honeymoon.'

"The next day, we were up early and reached the private airfield in good time.

"The young lady opened her small office at 8am and said,

'You are the only passengers so far but when we get twelve, we'll take off.'

"'Madam, what if you don't get 12 passengers?'

"'Then we will have to cancel,' she replied.

"'So, it's like the private Indian buses, shouting and calling for passengers and they only move, when they are full?'

"She didn't reply.

"My wife whispered, 'Have patience, it is a private jet!'

"At 8.30am, a young man walked in. 'Sorry I'm late,' he said. 'When's the flight taking off?'

"'We still need nine more passengers to fly today,' replied the lady.

"'Madam,' I asked, 'did anyone else show interest in travelling today?'

"'Yes, lots of people telephoned, but it depends if they turn up. I always tell them to report at 8am but you know the Indian standard time means anything up to two hours late.'

"At about quarter past nine, there was a commotion outside. A large family with rowdy children approached the office.

"The lady asked, 'How many are you?'

"'Including children, nine,' they replied.

"I jumped from my chair with joy.

"The lady called her manager. 'Sir, we have twelve passengers.'

"After about half an hour, she announced, 'OK, the plane's ready, let's go.'

"She took us through the small airfield where many small planes of various types were parked. The air hostess standing outside the 12-seater plane welcomed us and informed us, 'Unfortunately, the toilet facilities are not available in the flight. If anyone wants to avail themselves, can they use the airfield toilets please?'

"Once inside the plane, the air hostess took us through the flight-safety demonstration.

"'Please, make sure the children wear seat belts, they are not allowed to get out of their seats at all.'

"The pilot announced, 'The flight is one hour and thirty minutes.'

"I was sitting on the front row behind the pilot. After about forty minutes of travelling, the plane started shaking and a voice with an American accent came over: 'Danger, descend with caution! Danger, descend with caution!'

"Flashing red lights appeared on the dashboard panel above the pilot.

"I looked below from my window, there were mountain ranges. My heart jumped.

"I looked in front and the pilot was reading the *Times of India*.

"I could not control myself. 'Sir, please concentrate on flying.'

"'Don't worry, we have crossed Chandigarh, there are no weather problems.'

"'I am more worried about your aircraft problems, why is this voice saying danger...'

"'Just ignore this voice, it does it all the time,' said the pilot.

"'But why is it shaking so much?'

"'Because it is an old American aircraft,' replied the pilot.

"'How can you ignore a warning? It might be real this time.'

"The pilot picked the newspaper again.

"'No, please don't,' I shouted. 'We'll be news ourselves.'

"He threw the newspaper down.

"'Are we nearly there?' asked the children in the backseats. They repeated it again and again.

"Their grandfather shouted, 'No, we are not, can't you see? I am praying, only God will get us there.'

"The plane was shaking more and more. My hands were trembling, my heart beating faster and faster.

"After tightly holding my wife's hand, out of fear rather than love, for what seemed a long time, the pilot's voice came over. 'We are approaching Kullu Airport. The descent will start soon.'

"There was a big cheer from the children and everyone clapped. It was a smooth landing despite being a small aircraft.

"My heart returned to its normal rate and rhythm.

"I addressed the pilot. 'Sir, I am sorry for shouting at you. I was frightened.'

"He looked at the large red and white bangles on my wife's wrists and said, 'I see you are newly wed, I wish you a happy married life.'

"'Thank you, sir.'

"I told my wife, 'No more private jets. What a bumpy start to our honeymoon.' I managed to get a booking on a regular flight for the return journey.

"Relieved, she said, 'I hope we have no more turbulence on our honeymoon.'"

✵ 14 ✵

WRONG PLACE, WRONG TIME

The drums were beating loudly. People with red scarves tied around their heads were dancing to Bollywood tunes. There were red flags everywhere.

Sandip said, "Come on Taj, a street party. Let's join the celebrations."

Sandip started the bhangra dance with Taj.

The mood of the crowds changed when the speaker started chanting slogans.

"Down with the management, long live workers rights."

Taj could not understand. His eyes were watering, people were screaming and running helter-skelter.

Feeling a blow on his head, he fell down.

Lying on the ground, he looked up.

Bending over him was a policeman with a lathi stick in his hand. "Get out or I will arrest you, this march is illegal."

Taj was unsteady on his feet. He was coughing and spluttering.

People were fleeing the choking cloud of teargas. He saw

the fallen placards and realised that it was a workers' union demonstration.

On the way to the hospital in a taxi, Sandip put a handkerchief tightly on his brother's head to stop the bleeding.

Sitting next to him in the casualty department, a young man with a red headband introduced himself. "I am a union leader. I have never seen you on the factory floor?"

"I am a tourist. I was only a spectator."

"Oh, in that case I'm sorry. You were at the wrong place at the wrong time."

"What was this protest about?" enquired Sandip.

"Our trade-union leadership was invited by the management. Our union secretary was suspended two weeks ago when he asked workers not to work overtime unless paid extra. We went on strike. The management called us for a meeting. We thought the company wanted to reinstate our secretary and pay extra for overtime, our two main demands. But the company director was loud and aggressive. 'You and your men will starve, if you continue the strike.'

"Our union president shouted back, 'Learn to respect your workforce. We work hard so you can have a good life.'

"'I don't want lectures from my workers. I am your employer, I tell you what to do.'

"'You are dependent on us to run the factory. Agree to our demands or the strike continues.'

"'No, you are the thugs. You destroy the lives of workers who want to work.'

"'You insult us.'

"'I don't care for people like you, you are parasites who use workers for their own selfish ends.'

"Our union president got up and walked towards the company director and punched him in the face and left.

"The police arrested him. The company decided to close the factory until the workers returned to work and signed a clause ending trade-union membership.

"This demonstration was in protest against the company policy."

Taj needed five stitches on his scalp.

He was kept in casualty for two hours for head injury observations and then discharged with written instructions.

He said, "I always avoid big crowds in India but the drums and music was too enticing. I always thought, Indians celebrate life less but mourn death more but today, I saw a celebration of a union protest."

A month later, Taj read in the newspaper that the management decided to completely close the factory and relocate to another part of India.

The workers went on the rampage and set fire to the portion of the factory housing the machinery. The police opened fire and three workers were shot dead and many injured. What a violent end to an industrial dispute.

15

CLOSE ENCOUNTER

Taj was visiting his friend Amar, a university student in a small town near Delhi. To spend more time with his grandparents, Sandip decided not to accompany his brother.

At night, Taj stayed in his friend's rented accommodation. Abruptly woken from sleep from a loud bang, he opened the door. Four men came running in. They held a knife to both Taj and Amar's throat. They had hockey sticks. They all smelt of alcohol and one of them with trembling hands shouted at Amar.

"You bastard, you purposely hit my leg in the hockey match today. I'll teach you a lesson."

When the men were briefly distracted by the whistles from the neighbourhood watchman, Taj and Amar fled the house. They hid in the front garden bushes of one of their neighbour's houses. It was a dark, cloudy night. They heard the roar of two motorcycles going around the neighbourhood.

It was frightening when the motorcycles stopped just outside their hiding place.

They could hear them talking.

"We'll find them."

"They can't run for long."

"I want to see him bleed to death!"

"Don't worry, I'll hold him and you take your revenge."

Taj felt his heart jump. He almost stopped breathing with fear.

It seemed an eternity, but the motorbikes started again and they were gone. They waited until the first daylight and cautiously returned to their house, all the way looking over their shoulders. They locked all the doors and windows but were frightened to sleep.

"What's this about a hockey match?" asked Taj.

"I was playing fullback for my college team and he was centre forward for the local hockey club. I accidentally hit his shin with the hockey stick. He verbally abused me and threatened me," replied Amar.

"What happened then?"

"I shouted back, 'I'm not afraid of gangsters like you.' I came to know later on, he was indeed a dangerous gangster. I didn't expect him to come looking for me last night."

Amar knew a politician whom he telephoned in the morning and then visited his house, to request protection.

The politician said, "Don't worry, I have contacted an even bigger gangster!"

"You're sure I won't be attacked again?"

"Let me telephone this most powerful and respected gangster in town!"

"Good morning, sir."

"Did you sort out that hockey goon?"

"Yes, I sent my men and they have thrashed him and warned him that if he ever approaches Amar again, they will break his legs! He begged for mercy and promised he'll never touch Amar again."

Taj asked, "How could an accidental injury during a hockey match, cause a gang warfare leading to involvement of a politician?"

"Never ever call a gangster, a gangster, that's how it all started!" replied Amar.

16

A CASE OF PRIMITIVE BRAIN?

Mrs Sinha's son opened his mother's bedroom door in the morning to find her sitting in bed, looking distressed.

"What's wrong, mum?"

Tears rolled down her cheeks.

"Please tell me," the son pleaded.

She gestured him to bring pen and paper. She then wrote with trembling hands, "I cannot speak, please take me to hospital. I think I have suffered a stroke."

The Delhi hospital emergency department was heaving with hundreds of patients.

After a wait of three hours, the doctor saw his mother. He checked her thoroughly and told her, "I have found no neurological deficit."

"What does that mean?"

"I have found no defect in her neurological examination."

"So, my mother has not had a stroke?"

"No, I don't think so."

"Then why can't she speak?"

"I don't know. I will refer her to the Ear, Nose and Throat consultant."

The ENT specialist examined her and said, "Nothing is physically wrong on examination."

Mrs Sinha wrote on the paper, "I am shocked. You say everything is normal but I have completely lost my voice. I am not acting. I cannot speak at all."

The doctor replied, "It is probably due to stress and anxiety. You need to see a psychologist or a psychiatrist and also a speech therapist."

The son was very unhappy. "My mother is not mad; why should she see a psychiatrist? She was talking last night and this morning she could not talk at all. She is suffering a serious disease."

The doctor abruptly told the son, "I have ruled out serious illness. You are not helping your mother. We should reassure her."

"You have no empathy," yelled the son.

The doctor got up from his chair and said, "I see hundreds of patients in this busy casualty department. My job is to diagnose and treat them. I have no time for empathy. You can leave now."

The son remembered that his old friend Taj, a London psychologist, was visiting India.

In India, patients carry all their medical records themselves unlike in the UK, where the doctors keep them. Taj looked at the doctor's reports and told Mrs Sinha, "You don't seem to have had a stroke. I do believe you, that you are unable to speak and your suffering is real. You will need lots of speech therapy to help in the recovery of your voice."

"Why did my mother suddenly lose her voice if there is no disease causing it?"

"Has your mother suffered any emotional distress?" asked Taj.

"Not really."

"May I ask your father?"

Taj sensed the awkward silence in the room. "Mrs Sinha, are you able to tell me more about your husband? Please write on this paper."

Mrs Sinha began to write. *My husband telephoned me to tell me that he is going to live with another woman and is not coming home.*

"When did he telephone you?"

On the night of the loss of voice, she wrote

"Is my father responsible for this?" the son asked angrily.

"Our brain records everything but magnifies painful events in our lives. Sometimes, it can dramatically cause physical presentations like the sudden loss of speech. The good news is that with positive thinking, she can recover completely. Mind over body."

When Taj saw the smile on Mrs Sinha's face, he commented, "The recovery has already started."

Mrs Sinha's parents suggested she visit a holy man in their village they believed to do miracles. On visiting, the holy man asked Mrs Sinha to write down her thoughts on a paper and give it to her son. When the holy man told her what her thoughts were, the son was surprised as that was exactly what his mother had written on the paper. After blessing her, the holy man leaned forward and whispered something in her ear.

Then he said, "Have faith in God, Your speech will return completely."

After a month, Taj called Mrs Sinha's son and was amazed to hear of her full recovery. Upon further inquiry, he learnt that the son firmly believed that the speech returning had been thanks to a cure from the village holy man.

Intrigued, Taj visited the holy man, who lived in a small village hut.

Sitting crosslegged was a tall and skinny elderly man, with a long white beard.

He wore a saffron robe, had three horizontal parallel lines with a red mark across his forehead and a string of prayer beads in his hands. Taj knew religious men used these beads in meditation, to count the number of times a mantra was recited.

Some people were touching his feet and he was blessing them. Taj also took his blessings and sat on the floor.

"Sir, do you recall Mrs Sinha? You cured her. I am from London, please enlighten me?"

"Yes, we have a primitive brain deep inside our brain, that was affected in her case."

The holy man continued, "God created everything. He gave us blood in our bodies. Do you know the salt content in our blood is similar to salt in sea water? We have to remember God in our every breath. I taught her to do meditation of God."

"Are there any other cases you have cured?"

"Yes, there was a poor villager who was hit by a speeding car. He was in coma for a long time. When he came out of it, he started sniffing like a dog."

"Why was that?"

"The severe head injury affected his primitive brain. He had a heightened sense of smell like animals. As our primitive brain is spiritual, I taught him to meditate. When you are connected to God, all your problems are cured."

"Sir, are you able to cure cancer?" asked Taj.

The holy man closed his eyes.

The disciple told Taj, "No more questions. It's time for meditation."

Everyone was told to leave.

✤ 17 ✤

STREET VENDORS

Taj explained to Sandip, "You hear various voices on the streets in India. They sound similar but are in fact very different in their content.

"*Sabziwala* sells vegetables. *Fruitwala* sells fruit. *Raddiwala* buys newspaper and magazines from homes. They roam the streets on their bicycles or carts.

"The Raddiwala pay cash for the papers after weighing them. The humble raddiwala helps paper recycling in India. If you eat snacks from a tea shop, it will be wrapped in a newspaper, most probably bought by raddiwala."

It is estimated that there are 10 million street vendors in India, though they are increasingly threatened by the large shopping malls and supermarkets and many are harassed by the police for operating without a licence.

Taj met one vendor entrepreneur who occupied a space on the pavement in a residential neighbourhood. He loaned popular Indian magazines at half the price of a new magazine and by loaning to many customers, he made profit. He displayed his magazines on the street in the same place every day and was popular with students.

Taj's grandmother would buy fruit and vegetables from the cart of the same vendor every day. Taj loved the mangoes and papayas, the summer seasonal fruits.

The vendor told him that he visited the wholesale vegetable and fruit market at 4am where fresh vegetables and fruits arrived from the farms every day. This hardworking cart vendor was popular with the street residents.

One day, Taj and Sandip were visiting an area in old Delhi where there were hundreds of outdoor stalls selling everything from artworks to antique works. These stalls encroached on the pavement and every space inside was utilised. Some stalls were so full that the trader had to stand outside.

It was a noisy area with lots of shoppers. The stalls selling food were the most popular.

A friend once told Taj, "Bargaining is an art in India. You approach a vendor but pretend you are not interested. He calls you a friend and offers you a special price. It means that he is inflating the price and he is not your friend. Walk away, telling him that he is charging too much but don't wander far. He will shout a lower price but don't show interest. He will shout a further lower price. Go back to the vendor, complaining the price is still high. Persist with bargaining until you arrive at a mutually acceptable price."

A man standing outside a stall called out to Taj in good English, "We sell wood handicrafts of India which you will not get anywhere else and our prices are very reasonable."

Taj decided to take a look.

"They are famous handicrafts, the best in India," boasted the shopkeeper.

"Thank you. Sorry, but are they made in India or China?" asked Taj.

"India. Which country are you from?" asked the shopkeeper.

"The UK."

"I could guess from your British accent and because only English people say thank you and sorry. Please have a complimentary drink," said the shopkeeper.

"No thanks, I will come another time."

"Sir, please do me a favour, if you kindly put a good comment for my shop?"

"I am in a hurry now."

"Please sir, I would be grateful," he pleaded with folded hands.

The shopkeeper gave him a sheet of paper and Taj wrote on the comments section, "Interesting handicrafts." The shopkeeper pointed to the sections titled name, address and signature and requested Taj complete them.

On accidentally lifting the top sheet of paper, Taj found a sheaf of black carbon paper and underneath it an invoice with list of goods bought from the shop. The carbon paper would have transferred his name, address and signature to the invoice beneath. Taj quickly walked out of the shop, ignoring the protests from the shopkeeper.

"That was clever of you to lift the top sheet and discover the fraud," said Sandip.

"Now you know I'm the smarter brother."

Next day, the brothers were to travel to Bengaluru, previously called Bangalore.

✣ 18 ✣

TRAIN JOURNEY TO BENGALURU

Platform number 5 at Delhi railway station on a hot, humid August day was rather uncomfortable. The stall selling shikanjvi, a cooling Indian drink made from fresh lemon juice, was doing brisk business.

The coolies suddenly appeared, wearing bright red uniforms with brass armbands. They precariously balanced luggage on their heads. The loudspeaker blasted, "The train to Bangalore is 50 minutes late."

The coolies started leaving for other platforms where trains were due. Some passengers paid the coolies but others were unhappy.

"I agreed to pay after you put my luggage in my compartment."

"Madam, what can I do if your train is late?"

"I will pay you now, if you promise to come back when my train arrives."

Taj remembered being told by a friend if you need

information about train arrivals or departures and from which platform, ask a coolie.

Sandip was scratching his sweaty skin. He was paranoid about mosquitoes and being infected with malaria. He wondered how people were sleeping on the platform as if there were no flies or mosquitoes. Whenever Sandip heard the high-pitched buzzing of mosquitoes, he would clap his hands to kill them. The more he tried to wave them away, the more bites he suffered. "Why me, is it because I'm British?!"

At the tea stall, Taj drank tea from a clay cup. People were eating puris (deep fried Indian bread) with potato curry.

The train finally arrived, an hour late. Taj had booked a first-class air-conditioned sleeper cabin. It had four berths and the ticket collector checked their tickets and allocated the two lower berths to them. A young couple said that the upper berths belonged to them.

The man said that he was a businessman from Delhi. He said, "It takes thirty-six hours to reach Bangalore, a long journey. I am glad we have your company!"

He wanted to know everything about them. The four became very friendly and played cards together. Sandip felt at home with the young lady. He chatted with her all day and invited them to London. They exchanged mobile numbers as the train passed through small villages and farmers working in paddy fields.

Taj told Sandip, "Look outside, the scenic beauty of rural India, the stunning landscape, dotted with hills, rivers and streams."

When Sandip didn't reply, he looked at him and found him looking into the eyes of Monica, their fellow passenger.

Taj took him aside and advised him, "Behave yourself, she is a married lady."

"I'm sorry," Sandip replied, "but I feel really good when she's around."

The last night of journey, the couple shared their drinks with the brothers. Taj mentioned that he would ask the ticket collector to wake him before his arrival at Bangalore but the man said, "Don't worry, I'll wake you."

Taj bolted the cabin door from inside and felt safe. They said goodnight to each other and the young lady said, "Have sweet dreams, we will wake you up before Bangalore."

The brothers were surprised to be woken up by the ticket collector.

He said, "You sleep deeply, the train finished here in Bangalore."

They felt dizzy and drowsy. The wallets from their pockets and the rucksack containing their passports were gone. No trace of their luggage, either.

They told the ticket collector about their loss. He shrugged his shoulders and said, "These incidents are getting worse. You should have been more careful. They get friendly and spike drinks."

"Yes," Sandip said, "the drink made by the lady tasted different."

Taj said, "I wasn't even interested in that drink but she insisted. 'In the name of friendship, let's drink,' she said."

Sandip sighed. "I should never have trusted that woman. Oh wait, I have her mobile number." He tried the number but it was a fake.

Having cancelled their credit cards with their bank, they needed a police report to claim on their insurance.

The police officer said, "Be cautious, when someone offers you food and drink on a train."

Taj replied, "But officer, Indian hospitality is such that many passengers share their meals and even desserts with strangers. How can we be suspicious?"

"It's tricky, that's why these criminal gangs are successful," agreed the officer.

After questioning and the filling of forms, they were issued a police report.

With the report in his hands, Sandip said, "This is the end of our problems."

"Oh no, not yet, we will have to spend time at the British Consulate in Bangalore to obtain replacement documents in place of our lost passports," responded Taj.

"I felt really good with Monica. She fooled me completely, but I'm wiser now."

"Knowing you, when it comes to women, I don't think you'll ever learn," quipped Taj.

ॐ 19 ॐ

CHECK-IN

Sandip and Taj were checking in at the hotel reception in Bangalore.

"Can we take a copy of your passport and visa, please?"

"Here are the police reports regarding our lost passports."

"Can we see your Indian visa, please?"

"Sorry, we didn't realise we needed the visa. We left it with our grandfather in Delhi but we can ask him to send it online tomorrow. Lucky we didn't bring it, otherwise it would also have been lost."

"Sir, I apologise, I cannot check you in, without a copy of the visa."

"Can I see your manager?" said Taj unhappily.

"I understand your frustration, but the hotel has to give details of all foreign guests to the police by midnight every day," said the manager.

"The time now is 23:10 hrs. We can wait one hour and you

can check us in at 00:10 hrs. Our visa will be with you before your deadline of midnight tomorrow," suggested Sandip.

"OK then," the manager said reluctantly. "You promise to send me online proof of visa tomorrow."

An elderly gentleman was listening. He congratulated Sandip on his brilliant idea and introduced himself as Dr Mishra. He was a retired doctor from London and they sat down to have drinks.

"When I told my doctor friends in India that I have retired at the age of 60, they asked if I was crazy. 'You are wasting your medical experience. You will lose respect,' they said."

It seemed there was no concept of retirement in India. Here, it was associated with loss of respect and dignity.

Dr Mishra shared some funny thoughts about ageing.

"Everything goes thinner as you grow older. Hairs thin and fall. Skin thins and itches and wrinkles. Bones thin, causing fractures. If you suffer with osteoporosis, you lose your height also. The grey matter in the brain also thins. Now you tell me, do we wait for ageing to take its toll or retire and enjoy life without arthritic knees?"

Dr Mishra was full of humour with his jokes.

"English fathers say to their children, 'Go out in life and follow YOUR dream,' whereas Indian fathers say to their children 'Go out in life and follow MY dream; become a doctor!'

"An anxious Englishman says to his friend, 'I have been pickpocketed and lost my wallet and credit cards!'

"'Where did it happen?'

"'I was shopping in Chor Bazaar.'

"'What's the Chor Bazaar?'

"'It is the market where they only sell stolen goods.'

"'So you got mugged in the thief market!'"

Taj asked Dr Mishra, "Are you touring India?"

"No, I am doing charity work in India. I studied medicine in India but spent all my working life in the UK. After I retired, I felt that I had given all my service to the NHS but what about my service to my motherland? So, I joined a charity in India."

"What do you do?"

"I see patients in a small hospital in a rural, deprived area where a simple treatment like rehydrating powder saves children's lives. I see lots of tropical diseases and interesting cases."

Dr Mishra began talking about the case of a patient he had seen a few months ago.

"A man came in looking anxious. He spoke like a man who had accepted the fate of his imminent death: 'My family is cursed! We all die around the age of forty. Today I am forty years old. My father died at the age of forty, my two elder brothers died at the ages of forty two and forty three years.'

"Following blood tests, the results were shocking, even for such an experienced doctor like me. Cholesterol levels were very high, the bad cholesterol level was even higher. When the younger brother was tested, aged thirty four, similar blood results came back. In fact, they were all suffering with a condition called familial Hypercholesterolemia. Present from birth, and worsening with age, this condition causes premature deaths due to cardiovascular disease, usually occurring in the thirties or forties. Whole families become affected, given it is a genetic disorder, and it was a miracle that this man was still alive with working arteries.

"Both brothers were immediately started on high doses of

cholesterol-lowering drugs, resulting in their dangerous blood levels gradually coming down. It was such a satisfying experience to be able to save these brothers and break the so-called curse of death by screening the rest of the family too."

With a spark in his eye, remembering some of his most fascinating cases, Dr Mishra continued to tell his stories to Sandip and Taj.

Listening avidly, both had all but forgotten to check their watches and keep an eye on the time, no longer counting down the minutes until they could finally check in and turn in for the night. Dr Mishra took a sip of water to wet his throat and began again.

"In the same village one evening, around the same period, an older man came running to raise the alarm about his neighbour, a young man, behaving aggressively, shouting and swearing, without any provocation. Following him back to his home, the young man was stood outside his house watching those going past and shouting nonsensical profanities at them. His dirty red shirt was torn around his chest and his shoes had been kicked to one side. His eyes were bulging as he shouted, little flecks of spit flying around, showing his anger.

"However, as soon as he noticed someone approaching him directly, he sprinted inside his house, slammed the door and crawled under his bed. Trying to follow him inside was difficult. Pushing the door open gently revealed bits of broken pottery strewn across the floor. The curtains were half hanging off their rail, and it appeared as if the house had not seen any love or cleanliness in over a month. As he heard footsteps approaching him, his body began to tremble and there was a defensive look in his eye, like a mouse waiting for the cat to approach.

"His mouth began to form shapes, with odd sounds coming out. Saliva was dribbling from his mouth, and after a few moments, words became comprehensible. 'They are shooting, they are shooting at me!'

"Looking around, the room was empty, the rest of the villagers opting to wait outside.

"He pointed at the wall and whispered, 'Look, bullet marks.'

"Following his finger, nothing could be seen on the wall bar bits of flaky white plaster and the shadow of where a photo frame had once hung.

"He was sweating profusely with fear, droplets were forming on his brow and his shirt hung limply from his body, becoming increasingly drenched by sweat. And yet still he hugged himself tightly and trembled as if cold and shivering.

"The startling sound of broken pottery being pushed to one side and a shadow falling over the room revealed a man standing in the doorway. He took a look around before his eyes settled on the young man cowering under the bed, and his eyebrows knitted together in concern. In a flash, he had crossed the room, and knelt down to place a hand on the young man's head, stroking softly.

"'Ssh, in a few days we will go, we will find your cure, and rid you of this evil spirit, my son.' Turning slowly away from his son, but still gently stroking his hair, he whispered, 'This is my son, Harish. I thank you for coming Dr Mishra, but there is nothing you can do for him. He has been cursed by black magic, and I have been told the only way to break this is by travelling two days up into the mountains to see a holy man who can help."

"Harish began to whimper under the bed, grasping his father's hand tightly.

"He pulled his father towards him and with wide eyes fixated on a point on the wall, he said, 'They want to kill me. My food is poisoned, the air is poisoned, this house is laced with poison.'

"The father once more turned to his son, to whisper calming words in his ear and soothe his son's growing agitation.

"'My son has been hearing voices for the last few weeks. At first they were few and far between, but now they seem to be constant and ever more violent. He can't help his temperament, but it will be cured soon and I hope the rest of the village will understand and accept him once more.'

"Watching this exchange with admiration at this father's love and understanding for his son, it became clear that this was no black magic, but a psychotic illness in which visions can appear as real as everyday people as patients lose touch with reality.

"Looking back, when the old man came running for my help, he'd shouted, 'My neighbour is in the possession of a jinn. He is aggressive to everyone.'

"I thought he was talking about a man who was drunk with gin! But Jinn in some parts of India refers to a person who is possessed by spirits or demons."

Dr Mishra was interrupted by the bar attendant's voice. "We are closing in five minutes."

Taj looked at his watch and said, "Oh, it is nearly 1am, we should check in now.

Sandip asked Taj to check in and said he would join him later.

Sandip, more interested in the story, asked, "How is Harish now?"

"He helps his father on the farm," replied Dr Mishra. "His mental illness is now well controlled with medication."

Sandip asked, "How did you convince him to take medication rather than travel to see a holy man?"

"The villagers have lot of respect and trust for a doctor. If you educate them, they do follow your advice."

Sandip asked, "Why did you leave India for the UK?"

"Many Indian hospitals now are of international standard but then things were different. I wanted to do further medical training in UK and come back. Then, as my children were receiving education in England, I decided to continue staying there. The NHS treats all patients equally with respect and dignity. Let me tell you an amusing story from about forty years ago. Indian hospitals were then chaotic and understaffed.

"Often patients would have relatives sitting on their beds.

"One time, the nurse mistakenly gave a relative sitting on patient's bed an enema despite his protestations, saying, 'doctor's orders, you cannot refuse.'

"In the evening, the consultant did the ward round. The patient was still complaining of tummy pains but the smiling relative thanked the doctor, "I feel great after your nurse gave me the enema. My constipation is cured!

20

BENGALURU VISIT

Taj and Sandip were in Bangalore, sitting on the balcony of their room on the third floor, enjoying the warm morning sunshine. The birds were chirping from the overhanging branches of tall trees.

The serenity started getting increasingly interrupted as the traffic started building up on the main road below their hotel.

The unending honking of cars, scooters, auto rickshaws and trucks became a nuisance. It seemed that there was a competition as to who was the loudest and the longest hooter.

Sandip noticed the chaos on the nearby roundabout. It was like the British special Air Service SAS motto, "Who dares wins." The drivers raise their hands to tell others to stop and then accelerate their cars forward.

Taj told Sandip, "Look, there's a cow walking on the fast lane. Now I know why grandad says prayers before setting out on the roads. When you share the road with sacred cows, overloaded lorries, errant rickshaws and scooter drivers weaving in and out of lanes at top speed, you need God on your side."

Behind their hotel, there were massive buildings, looking like palaces with security guards. On enquiring, they found out that these buildings were the famous call centres of Bangalore.

Sandip said, "These call centres are well protected. What about our protection from them? They invade our privacy in our homes in UK with uninvited calls that ask,

'You were involved in an accident?'

'No, not I am aware of.'

'It was not your fault.'

'How could it be my fault, when I have never had an accident?'

'Think again, it could be a workplace accident in the last three years?'"

Sandip thought of all the calls back home from call centres. He always wondered why people in these centres had English names despite their typically Indian accent.

Taj corrected Sandip, "You are describing cold calls. In fact, call centres in Bangalore do work outsourced to them by big respectable companies of the USA and the UK. The best software engineers in the world come from Bangalore, the IT hub of India."

Sandip was surprised to learn that the city of Bangalore had over five hundred pubs.

He peered into some of them, amazed how the atmosphere was quite similar to his own favourite stomping ground in London. But on further observation, he realised the big difference here was the strong aroma of food and every table had more food than drinks.

They also visited an interesting Parsee restaurant. It served Parsee meals and educated customers about the history and customs of the Parsee people. The walls of the restaurant were covered with such stories.

The Parsees are followers of the Persian Prophet Zoroaster. They fled to India from Iran to avoid religious persecution between the 8th and 10th century following the Arab conquest of Persia (Iran).

Taj was surprised to read that dead Parsees do not have burial or cremation. They are taken to the towers of Silence, which are circular raised structures where dead bodies are exposed to rays of the sun and to the birds of prey. The reason given for this practice is that Earth, Fire and Water are considered sacred elements which should not be defiled by the dead. The population of Parsees in India is about 60,000. They worship at the Fire Temples. They have made considerable contributions to the history and development of India, which is all the more remarkable considering their small numbers.

Taj asked Sandip, "Which Indian Parsee family plays a significant role in the British economy?"

"I don't know."

"The Tata family. They are well-known industrialists in India and are owners of Tata Motors and also run Jaguar Land Rovers in the UK."

There was a story that more than 1000 years ago, 500 Parsi families landed in Gujarat, India from Iran. They did not speak the local language and so Jadi Rana King of a tiny principality in Gujarat showed them a bowl of milk filled to the brim to demonstrate that his country was full and could not accommodate more. The Parsee priest put a pinch of sugar into the milk which immediately dissolved without overflowing the bowl of milk. With this action, he symbolised that accepting the Zoroastrians would add sweetness to the country without upsetting the population.

Sandip said, "It reminds me of Brexit in UK."

The Parsees had to agree to two conditions that they adopt the local language and their women wear the local dress, the sari, before they were granted permission to stay by the king.

When they came out of the restaurant, on the streets outside people were dancing to the playing of huge drums. It was the twenty-fifth of August and Bangalore was in a festive spirit. Men wore traditional clothes with saffron cloth tied around their heads. Saffron is a sacred colour for the Hindus. Even the rain could not dampen their spirits; it was the Shri Ganesha festival.

Ganesha has a human body and an elephant's head. Ganesha is revered in Hinduism as the remover of obstacles and deva of intellect and wisdom. It is the most worshipped deity. There were idols of Ganesha everywhere, some small and some very big in the stalls. People were taking the idols home for worship in their cars and the big idols in their vans. Taj and Sandip were invited to a farmhouse for Ganesha worship.

It was a beautiful ceremony of prayers followed by a delicious meal and different types of desserts made with coconut, which were all very colourful and tasty.

When Taj filled his plate second time with the desserts, Sandip raised an eyebrow.

"Eat until overfull is the custom in India." Taj whispered.

They were shown around the farm. Taj was surprised to learn that avocados grown on the farm were fed to the cattle until a few years ago when they came to know that avocados were the fruit of celebrities and had huge health benefits. People started selling them and making good profits.

That night, the brothers slept early as next morning they were travelling to Pondicherry.

21

PONDICHERRY

Pondicherry, a popular tourist destination on the south east coast of India, was the setting for the Oscar winning Hollywood film *Life of Pi*, based on the Booker prize-winning novel by Yann Martel.

It was an early morning flight and they caught the taxi to Bengaluru airport. Taj sat on the front passenger seat and Sandip on the rear seat. Taj noticed that the taxi was being driven in and out of their lane. He looked at the driver, who had nodded off. Coming round a corner, their taxi was going to hit an oncoming car. He lurched forward towards the steering wheel.

Hands wet with sweat on the wheel, panting heavily, Taj steered the taxi safely.

The driver opened his eyes.

"Stop the car now," shouted Taj.

The taxi stopped. Taj gave the driver water. He drank and also splashed water on his eyes. He reassured them that he was fully awake now. So, they started again.

The car suddenly hit the kerb on the side of the road. The driver had nodded off again.

The car stopped. Taj thought that the tyres had burst but luckily they were intact. The driver apologised and promised that he would drive safely.

Taj said, "No, never. I don't trust you. I will drive myself."

Finally, the driver gave his keys to Taj.

Sandip told Taj, "You don't have insurance. Why take the risk?"

Taj replied, "I rather take that risk than lose our lives if we let this man drive us."

They safely reached the airport.

The driver folded his hands and said, "Please don't complain to my taxi company, they'll sack me and there will be no food on the table for my three young children and my two wives."

"Two wives? No wonder you're sleepy while driving," exclaimed Taj. "I'll pay the full fare but you are a danger on the roads."

After check-in, Taj realised that he had left his mobile in the taxi.

He went to the information desk and explained to the receptionist. She rang the taxi company and was told that the taxi was still at the airport.

The young lady said, "I'm not supposed to leave this desk but I'll quickly run and find your mobile in the taxi."

The brothers waited anxiously as boarding was in thirty-five minutes and they still had to get through security.

Sandip told Taj, "Let's go, we'll miss our flight if you go on waiting for your mobile."

Taj looked at his watch and at the airport entrances. With no sign of the lady, Taj decided to go without his mobile.

There was a shout as he turned around. "Sir wait, I have it."

Taj thanked her and said apologetically. "Sorry, I was worried if it takes time in the security, I would miss my flight."

"Don't worry," she said. "I'll lead you to the fast lane for the security."

Taj said, "I have never seen such exceptional customer service at the airport."

They went through the security gate and waited for their hand luggage.

The officer shouted, "Whose bag is this?"

Sandip looked at the bag. "It's mine."

The officer said, "Open the bag."

"But we'll miss our flight."

"Sorry, I have to do my job. Please show me the contents of the bag."

Sandip quickly emptied the bag.

The officer took his time checking all the contents.

He then picked the hand-cream tube and said, "You should have carried this tube in a transparent plastic bag."

Only fifteen minutes left for boarding. Sandip quickly threw all the things back into his bag.

Taj looked at the screen. "Boarding gate 19. Last reminder."

They started running. Taj was breathless. Gate 19 seemed so far but he was relieved to see Sandip at the boarding gate, waving at him. They were the last passengers to board the plane.

The pilot announced, "The flight to Pondicherry is one hour and ten minutes."

Taj said, "What an eventful beginning to our trip."

Sandip laughed. "What do you reckon are the chances of our pilot having two wives too?!"

Taj replied, "I hope not. I don't want him sleeping in the cockpit."

In Pondicherry, on the way to their holiday resort, they crossed a village with small houses, some with big carved wooden doors.

The taxi driver pointed. "These houses belong to families whose sons have emigrated to France and send money from there and the parents proudly install expensive doors to make the neighbours jealous."

Sandip wondered why France but was embarrassed to ask.

Now, they were approaching their resort.

It was surrounded by lush green farms and hundreds of coconut trees.

After checking in at the resort reception, they sat on the balcony of their first-floor sea-view room. The fresh breeze from the sea felt pleasant on a hot sunny summer day. There were small fishing boats on the sea.

Sitting on the branch over their balcony, a crow was cawing loudly.

Looking down, there were rabbits running all over the grounds of the resort. Some were munching grass. A lady with a broomstick appeared. She was chasing the rabbits to their enclosure. One cute pink rabbit hid in the bushes under their room. The lady approached the rabbit and hit him with the stick. It jumped and ran towards the rabbit enclosure.

She locked the gate after all the rabbits got in.

"She hurt that rabbit!" exclaimed Sandip. "I'm complaining to the resort management."

"I don't think she hurt him. She probably hit the ground near him," said Taj.

After a long tiring day, the brothers decided to walk along the sea. The resort path leading to the beach was lined with trees and shrubs.

It was sunset time. A ball of fiery red glow was descending on the sea horizon. The stray dogs were busy fighting on the sandy beach.

Sandip told Taj, "let's go for a jog and get rid of some calories."

Taj resisted, knowing he was a poor runner, but Sandip insisted.

Taj heard a bark behind him and when he looked, he was being chased by a group of dogs.

Far ahead, Sandip was surprised when Taj overtook him. He had never seen him run so fast.

"What happened," shouted Sandip.

"The ferocious looking dogs are chasing me."

"There are no dogs behind you."

Taj turned and looked back.

Relieved, he stopped, but it took him ten minutes to recover.

He said to Sandip, "I'm exhausted. Let's go back and end this stressful day."

Early next morning, they went for a stroll along the beach.

Sandip promised Taj no jogging today.

From behind the clouds rose the sun, casting a golden line of reflection on the water.

Sandip said, "It looks like the sun is extending a golden handshake to people on the beach. It feels so serene."

When the waves came in, it was fun watching the crabs

burrowing and hiding in tiny holes in the sand.

When the water receded, they came out but being sandy coloured, careful observation was required to spot them.

Finally it was time for breakfast. They had never seen so many dishes. There were South Indian dosas, vadas and idli, North Indian Punjabi parathas, chole bhature, full English and continental breakfast.

"I think I have been overeating in India," said Taj, looking at his belly.

After breakfast, they decided to explore the history of Pondicherry.

First stop was the Museum. It depicted the history of Anglo-French wars in Pondicherry in 1742 to 1763. Pondicherry changed hands frequently but when the British gained control of India in the late 1850s, they allowed the French to retain the region. It remained a French colony until 1954 when it became part of independent India. The brothers were surprised that French was still spoken, along with Tamil and English.

Sandip said, "Just imagine, the beach we were walking on this morning, was the site of fighting between British and French forces."

Walking in the French Quarter, they saw the villas in French architectural style, painted bright pink, yellow and peach. The streets had French names and French cafes.

Reading from his guide book, Sandip said, "Wow this church was originally built by Napoleon in 1855 and is believed to be based on Notre-Dame in Paris."

Then, they visited the Hindu Ganesha temple, with its long queue of devotees waiting to pay respect to the deity of Lord Ganesha. There was an information board depicting the history of the temple.

It said the French tried to put the deity into the sea of the Bay of Bengal three times but every time the devotees managed to rescue it. The French governor finally gave in and allowed the deity to be installed in the Ganesha temple.

It was an educational trip, but tiring in the hot sun.

On the way back in a taxi, they stopped at a fruit stall.

The stall holder said, "These are papayas from our farm, the coconuts are fresh from the trees."

"What about these small green bananas?" asked Sandip.

"Definitely fresh from our farm. No fertilisers used. They will turn yellow tomorrow, ready to eat."

And the next morning, they were indeed yellow and delicious, better than any organic banana in the UK.

Pondicherry is famous for its association with an Indian spiritual philosopher, Sri Aurobindo.

After breakfast, they visited Sri Aurobindo ashram. People were meditating in silence. It was a very tranquil place.

Next, they took the taxi to Auroville, a universal township dedicated to the vision of Sri Aurobindo. They could not get the tickets to enter the township. So, they walked to a viewing point where they could see a golden sphere structure. They were told that it was called Matri mandir. It was the centre for meditation. The brothers were surprised to learn that the township, dedicated to world peace and tranquility, houses travellers from more than fifty countries.

"Pondicherry would be a worthy Olympic host with all these nationalities," said Sandip.

They returned to their resort in the afternoon, Taj experiencing pains in his lower back and legs.

Sandip said, "Look, the resort has Ayurveda massage for body pains."

Taj reluctantly agreed and they visited the spa to find the male receptionist there did the massage also.

He said, "My name is Mr Shankar. I can do Podikizhi massage to help your body and joint pains due to arthritis."

Sandip said, "No, my brother does not suffer with arthritis. It is obesity due to his patriotic love for fried Indian food."

He ignored Sandip and led Taj to the room with incense sticks and burning candles and asked him to undress and lie on a table.

He said, "I will do a full body massage with medicated oils, prepared according to the ancient Ayurvedic texts." He poured warm oil on his head and then on the hands, neck, back, chest and legs. He massaged the whole body in rhythmic motions. "Now I'm going to massage you with a medicated powder held inside a linen-cloth bundle."

"Where does the powder come from?" asked Taj.

"From the roots of special plants which grow in the forests of Kerala."

The cloth soaked in warm oil was tapped with lot of pressure on the stomach.

"Will it get rid of my belly? Burn my fat?"

Mr Shankar had a burning candle in his hands.

Taj arched away.

Mr Shankar said, "Sorry sir, I was not bringing it near you. One of the burning candles had fallen down so I had just picked it up. Sir, please lie on your stomach."

The table was so oily and slippery that Taj felt he would fall.

"Hold my hands when changing posture or getting up," said Mr Shankar.

Covered with oil from head to the soles of his feet and

with the massage completed, Taj was relieved to get off the table.

Mr Shankar said, "Do not take a bath straightway. Please sit in the sun for one hour."

☙❧

SITTING ON THE BALCONY, SANDIP LOOKED AT TAJ AND said, "Covered in oil, you look really fat."

"Shame on you, insulting your brother in front of Mr Shankar, calling me obese. Learn the respect which is given to elder brothers in India."

"I said the truth about your love for the fried stuff. You are obese. Check your body mass index. I bet you are way above the normal range."

"No, I just got the bad genes."

"Oh yes, scapegoat your parents and grandparents instead of improving your lifestyle."

"Shut up, I am spending my hard-earned money on this holiday, not like you, enjoying yourself on our parents' money."

Sandip walked away angrily.

After his shower, Taj couldn't find Sandip in the room.

He came to the balcony and looked down at the grounds. And there was Sandip, laughing with the joyful children among so many rabbits.

The children wanted to play with the rabbits but they jumped and ran away as soon as they were approached. Sandip was taking photos of the rabbits.

Taj shouted, "Sandip, look behind you, there's that pink rabbit."

And this time, it was Sandip who was jumping with joy. He had managed to catch the elusive pink rabbit in his selfie.

Dinner with the candle-lights under the open sky, with the band playing at the side of the swimming pool, was the most relaxing moment of their holiday.

The food was delicious. The music was entertaining. Taj just wished there was a woman in his life to share this with.

Next day, they were travelling back to Bengaluru.

Before leaving for the airport in the morning, they visited the resort shop and bought some gifts. They picked the silk scarves, candle holders and an embroidered bag. They went to the reception to check out and were told that their taxi was waiting.

On the way to the airport, a bus had broken down in the middle of the road, blocking the traffic. On the side of the bus, there was a sign. *Pondicherry Engineering college.*

The taxi driver said, "These engineering students should be able to move the bus."

As they were slowly pushing the bus to the side, a long line of traffic was edging forward from opposite sides of the road. Even their taxi driver was tapping impatiently on the steering wheel and inching forward. The bus had partly blocked the way but the cars now fully blocked the road.

Sandip said, "It's crazy, no one wants to give way, all they are doing is blowing their horns incessantly."

Suddenly, a traffic cop appeared.

Taj said, "Look, the cop narrowly escaped being knocked down by the scooters zig zagging around the cars."

The traffic police officer blew his whistle. The drivers on both sides of the road stared at him angrily as if to say, "Give the red card to the other side."

Taj said, "It is now one-way traffic at one time and we should be allowed first as there are heavy trucks behind us."

It seems the traffic cop agreed with him. He directed the opposite traffic to move back and give way.

Sitting on the wall next to the road, was a red-faced monkey. As a hawker, pushing a cart, laden with yellow bananas, got distracted in the chaos on the road, the monkey jumped, picked a banana and was quickly back on the wall.

Sandip said, "Look how the monkey has peeled the banana from the bottom, pretty cool. Oh no, he has thrown the banana skin on the pavement and someone is going to fall on that."

Amongst the cars sounding their horns and the cop whistling, the traffic had started to move.

Taj said, 'This is what you call organised chaos of Indian roads!"

At last, they had reached the airport.

Taj said, "This was the most relaxing part of our Indian trip. I'm glad we came."

"Pondicherry does have an aura of spirituality," agreed Sandip.

Sandip bought a book about Sri Aurobindo's thoughts at the airport.

It said, "Pain and pleasure are the same thing. They are just differently reproduced in the sensations and emotions. At the root of the malady lies our separation from the soul."

Sandip asked Taj to explain what it meant.

"I'll tell you once I find my soulmate," replied Taj with a smile.

It was time to fly back to Bangalore.

KERALA BACKWATERS

The brothers and their friend Pavan landed in Kochi airport to visit Kerala, also called God's own country. The brothers travelled from Bangalore while Pavan from Bhopal had to get a flight from Delhi.

They learnt about the old spice trade, saw the Chinese fishing nets used for centuries by the fishermen and visited India's oldest Synagogue built by the Jewish community in the 16th century.

Taj booked a houseboat online to see Kerala Backwaters. They paid Rs 60000 and were told by email to arrive no later than 11am. Taj emailed back to ask how they would recognise their houseboat. No reply came.

They left the city of Kochi in time and reached their destination before 11am.

There were so many houseboats looking for customers. Some of the boats looked majestic and charged Rs 30000, which was half of what they had paid.

On being telephoned, the agent said he was waiting for the boat.

Pavan suffered from photosensitive skin and the hot sun caused itchy rashes to break out. If they didn't find a houseboat soon, he would get badly burnt.

At 1pm, Taj telephoned again and was told the boat was being prepared and the agent couldn't tell how long it would take. There was no sign of the boat and it was 2pm. The midday sun was hot and uncomfortable. Taj telephoned the agent.

"Where is your boat?"

"Getting ready."

"You have not provided the service for which I have paid. I demand my money back."

"The money is non-refundable."

"I'll cancel the payment," shouted Taj.

"The money will not be returned. The credit-card company cannot cancel payment without my consent."

Taj had enough of waiting. In frustration, he telephoned the credit-card provider and explained the situation and asked for a refund. The customer advisor was not helpful.

Taj said, "Under section 75 of the consumer credit act, you are responsible as the service advertised online has not been provided."

"You can submit a claim for a refund and the credit card company will look into it," said the advisor.

They inspected a few boats and hired one, which was luxurious and cost only Rs 25,000.

The smartly dressed captain was a polite gentleman. He told Taj that his previous agent took excessive money from tourists and waited until he got a much cheaper boat, hence the tourists had to wait many hours.

It was a relaxing boat ride on palm-fringed waterways passing along lovely villages and rice paddies. The onboard cook made fresh hot dishes for every meal. The fish curry was especially delicious.

On the way, the boat stopped and the cook took them to a village to select fresh giant prawns. They sat on the deck under the night stars and chatted late into the night. Taj told Pavan about his African adventure. He was driving at night in his Volkswagen when he saw a rhino run right in front of his car. He was saved by a few inches by swerving to the other side.

At the time, there was an army coup in East Africa and the borders were closed. "There were soldiers with machine guns everywhere. I was very nervous when we reached the border at night. Me and my friend were told at gunpoint by three soldiers to get out of the car and escorted to the tent where their officer was sitting. My heart was racing and my hands trembling. The officer was drunk, he was struggling to get up from the chair. His voice was so slurred, I could barely understand him. Then, he shouted at me to show my passport.

"He held my passport upside down and looked at my photo and said in Swahili 'picha ako mazuri sana', meaning *your photo is very good*. He said this with a smile on his face and waving the gun in his hand. We were relieved when he allowed us to cross the border. My friend later told me he was almost going to tell the officer that he was holding my passport wrong.

"I said 'Thank God, you didn't, he would have shot us both!'"

It was time to retire to their cabins for the night.

Early morning, chirping birds woke Taj. He could hear the

sound of water lapping against the boat. He went on the deck. A light and pleasant wind was blowing. The trees on the sides of the river were moving gently in the breeze.

There was sunrise to see and lots of fishing boats passing by.

Tea and breakfast was served on the deck.

The boat stopped. It was a farm with coconut trees everywhere.

They came off the boat and sipped tender coconut water served in the coconut shell.

Sandip told Taj, "Look, birds having a free ride on the buffaloes."

Taj replied, "Nothing's free in this world. Birds eat ticks and other parasites that live on the skin of buffaloes. In return, buffaloes move bugs and insects, providing food for the birds."

"You're right," said Sandip. "The birds hover around the buffaloes and where they clear the ground, they seem to be feeding. Nothing's free in this world."

✿ 23 ✿

MEMORIES ON A BEACH

There were hundreds of people on a beach with lots of eating places in the state of Tamil Nadu in south India.

Taj was attracted to a massive dosa which was being cooked in the open on the seafront. Dosa is a south Indian dish – a kind of pancake made from fermented batter. Its main ingredients are rice and black gram.

The size of this dosa was about twenty times the normal size. It could easily cover a table seating fifteen to twenty people.

Taj was impressed. He asked the cook if something could be done about the flies sitting on the dosa.

The cook replied, "Don't worry sir, the flies are included in the price of this big family Dosa!"

Sandip, true to his cleanliness OCD, told Taj, "No way, let's go."

Taj reluctantly followed Sandip.

Nearby, children returning from camel rides on the beach

screamed during the bumpy dismount.

Further down the beach, some people were doing yoga on a raised platform.

The instructor was telling them, "Breathe in and focus on your bellies, rising like the waves on the sea."

Watching them, Sandip laughed. "Yes, they have big bellies and they do rise like big waves."

The sign on the seafront said: "Danger, Do not swim."

Taj's mind wandered to a similar sign he had seen when he visited Cape Verde Island on the west African coast. He had taken part in an organised trip to see lemon sharks. The guide was a marine biologist who said lemon sharks were mainly fish eaters and everyone would be safe.

A man in the group said, "lemon sharks are big and have sharp teeth. What if they confuse us for a type of fish!"

The guide was very reassuring. They waded into the sea for about 50 yards and stood in knee-deep water. Suddenly, sharks fins appeared. They were only about 20 to 30 yards away, and disappeared quickly. The guide said that the sharks would see them as shadows and they could scan the surroundings, which would show that they were standing at one place and no threat to them. They stood for about 30 minutes and at one stage, saw quite a few sharks. Taj noticed that when the group was walking towards the beach, the sharks seemed to come nearer. It was an unforgettable experience.

At the end of the beach was a lit-up toilet sign. Paying a visit, Sandip found no soap in the facility. He asked an Indian gentleman where he could get some.

The man opened his wallet. "Here's a paper-soap strip."

"You carry soap with you?"

"Yes, lots of people do that."

Sandip was impressed. "Where can I buy these soap strips?"

"Oh, in any shop."

"At the railway station?"

"Sure."

Sandip loved buying paper-soap strips from a local shop and carrying them in his wallet.

Taj joked, "Your credit card must be wondering why there's soap next to it."

"Because there's so much dust in India!" replied Sandip.

On the way back, they drove through the lush green countryside with coconut trees everywhere. The taxi driver stopped at a stall. The roadside vendor cut open the coconut and served them fresh coconut water. He then removed the cream from the inside lining of the coconut, which tasted slightly salty but delicious.

Taj said, "Look there, the black crows are gorging on the bright mangoes on the trees."

Sandip pointed out the ripening red bananas in the green fields and said, "The south Indian countryside is beautiful."

Further down the road, their driver suddenly braked. Sitting in the middle of the road was a group of monkeys.

The driver honked repeatedly but the monkeys didn't move.

Sandip got out of the taxi to stretch his legs. He opened his favourite packet of Walkers crisps, put one in his mouth and froze. The monkeys were running towards him. He panicked, his crisps fell down. He quickly got into the taxi.

They drove off. Sandip looked back. The monkeys were eating his crisps.

"Enjoy my London crisps!" he exclaimed.

❧ 24 ❧

A MYSTERY ILLNESS

T aj was visiting his long-standing friend Vijay and his wife, Seema.

On his first night, he heard heated arguments from their bedroom.

It seemed Vijay was losing money in his business and he was going to loan sharks, who were charging him exorbitant rates.

Seema pleaded with him, "Please close the business instead of taking more and more loans and getting further and further into debt."

"You only want me to be a failure!" Vijay shouted.

That morning, Taj was woken by screams from Vijay's bedroom. "Call the doctor, call the doctor."

Taj ran into their room. Vijay said in a tearful voice, "Seema cannot move her legs. Oh God, I hope she hasn't had a stroke."

Seema's speech was fine. She said, "I can't feel my legs."

They called the ambulance and she was admitted to the

hospital. The physician checked her and reassured Vijay that he did not find any abnormality. He arranged blood tests. The next day, Seema still couldn't move her legs. The neurologist did a thorough medical examination and arranged an MRI scan and electrical study of the nerves.

The neurologist told Seema and Vijay, "All the tests have come back normal, her neurological examination has not revealed any abnormality. In my opinion, there is no physical cause."

"And what other cause could it be?" asked Vijay.

"It could be due to mental stress," replied the neurologist.

"You think my wife is mad? She is suffering so much and you think it is all in her mind?"

The consultant reassured them, "Seema's illness is not fake and she will get better. She will need physiotherapy and help from the psychiatrist."

She was discharged from the hospital. Vijay refused to take Seema to the psychiatrist but instead took Seema in a wheelchair to his village. His parents convinced Seema that this was due to witchcraft. They took her to a Sadhu. He was a holy man who lived in a cave outside the village.

Seema touched his feet. He was tall with wavy hair, a long white beard and a wrinkled face but his eyes were bright. He was sitting in an upright yoga posture. He had a large red mark on his forehead. The story was that when he was a young man, he had a vision that he had to leave everything he loved. The next day he left his family and possessions and became homeless. He met a Guru in the mountains who taught him that inflicting pain on himself was the first step towards self realisation. He kept one arm raised over his head and meditated for long periods.

Despite the pain, he kept the same arm raised over many months causing it to become thin and deformed.

He had a peacock feather in his good hand which he waved over Seema's head to signify his blessings. The sadhu closed his eyes, repeated religious mantras and told her, "Start walking and if you fall, get up and walk like a child who falls again and again but never gives up."

On Taj's insistence, Seema did daily physiotherapy. The strength in her legs slowly returned and she could walk with an aid after about three months. But Vijay was convinced that the recovery was due to the Sadhu's blessings.

Seema asked Taj, "You are a psychologist, what do you think happened to me?"

He told her: "Mind and body are not separate, they need to work together. The subconscious mind is very powerful. If it is affected by severe stress, the ability to move the body could also be affected."

Seema nodded, it seemed in agreement.

Two years later, Taj met Vijay and Seema again. They had become proud parents of a baby girl.

Taj asked Seema, "How are you?"

Seema replied "We are happy now but it has been quite a journey. We sold our house to pay back the loan sharks. The bank agreed to allow us to pay back in instalments which we are still doing. I started helping Vijay in his business, which fortunately started making a profit."

Then came the pressure from her mother in law to have a child.

She even accompanied Seema to see a gynaecologist.

She said, "Doctor, they have not been successful in having a child despite trying for many years."

The gynaecologist checked Seema and arranged blood tests. "I need to check your husband at the next appointment."

Her mother-in-law intervened. "My son is healthy, you only need to investigate Seema."

The gynaecologist told them that a third of all cases of infertility are due to men. "I cannot proceed until I check your son."

Vijay reluctantly agreed.

On the next appointment, they were shocked. "Vijay, I am sorry, your sperm test shows no sperm," said the gynaecologist.

Vijay had the test repeated at another clinic and the result of "No Sperm" was devastating.

The gynaecologist gave different options including the use of a sperm donor.

Vijay's mother said, "It would not be our flesh and blood." She advised Vijay not to agree.

But remembering the stroke-like attack Seema suffered due to stress, Vijay agreed to a sperm donor.

"Everything is good now. The baby has brought so much happiness in our life," beamed Seema.

❧ 25 ❧
YOGIS

In India, Taj met a man who had spent some time in the Himalayas.

He said, "There are many people who meditate and do yoga in the Himalayas and reside in the caves. Some of them are over one hundred years old but have the energy of young people. They sit with hardly any clothes in the freezing temperatures and meditate for many hours."

"How can they survive?" quizzed Taj.

"They have attained a higher level of consciousness. They control their core body temperature. They can also control their breathing and even their heart rate."

Taj enquired, "How does one attain a higher level of consciousness?"

"By meditating in the name of God. When you control your mind instead of it controlling you, everything is possible. I returned home before I could achieve that."

"How come?"

"Early morning, every day, I used to touch the feet of

meditating sadhus as a mark of respect. One sadhu opened his eyes. 'Son, go home, your wife is going to die soon.'

"He was sitting cross-legged. He wore seven rows of beads around his neck. His dark skin was covered with ashes. His black hair was long, tied in a bun at the back of his head. He was naked except for the beads and the ashes.

"I panicked and managed to telephone home. My wife said, 'I'm fine but please come home, we all miss you.'

"When I reached home, I discovered she had suffered a massive heart attack and was poorly in hospital. I quickly proceeded to the hospital. She was breathless, fighting for her life. I held her hands until the doctor told me, 'I am sorry, your wife has died.'"

He continued, "I have always wondered how that sadhu in the mountains knew that my wife was going to die soon?"

Taj became interested in the relationship between yoga, the meditation and the mind. A yoga teacher told him that yoga stops the fluctuations of the mind and provides inner peace. Taj decided to study the subject.

Yoga is a group of physical, mental and spiritual practices or disciplines which originated in ancient India. The word yoga was first mentioned in the oldest sacred texts, the Vedas. The Vedas are the oldest writings in Hinduism. The beginnings of Yoga were developed by the Indus-sarasvati civilisation in northern India over 5,000 years ago. In ancient times, yoga was mostly spiritual practices revolving around core values.

The first value involved analysing one's own perceptions and cognitive state, understanding the root of suffering and using meditation to solve it. The mind was to transcend bodily pain or suffering in order to reach a higher level of being. The second value aimed to uplift or broaden consciousness.

Yoga in the western world is increasing in popularity. Now, even gyms use yoga to improve our health. Scientific studies have shown yoga reduces cardiovascular risk. In the scientific research paper in 2012 titled *how yoga works*, the hypothesis was that yoga works by regulating the nervous system by increasing the vagal tone. The Vagus nerve is the largest cranial nerve in the body, influencing the respiratory, digestive and nervous system. It regulates all our major bodily functions.

Once Taj heard an interesting conversation between a plumber and a doctor at the yoga centre.

The doctor said, "You use a spirit level to check if a surface is level or not. Similarly, our brain continually monitors the level of fluid in the semicircular canals in our inner ears, keeping our bodies balanced. That's why we can perform the difficult postures in yoga."

The plumber laughed. "The brain is the best plumbing system in the world. So, we are like doctors."

The doctor replied. "You sure are. We do an operation, the post-operative blood clot can cut off the blood supply causing death, your repair work on the pipes can cause an air bubble in the water pipes, cutting off the water supply."

A yoga session with medical learning!

❧ 26 ❧

WHAT A RIDE

The sun blazed down as the brothers enjoyed cool glasses of nimbu pani. The vendor squeezed fresh limes and made the drinks. Sandip had his salty and Taj preferred it sweetened.

They were sitting outside a food outlet in a noisy bus station. The waiter cleaned their dusty table with a dirty, food-stained cloth before bringing their order of fried puris and white chickpeas in a curry.

Sandip said, "The food is hot and delicious."

Taj told him, "I noticed that you didn't comment on the dirty cleaning cloth. You were so hygiene conscious when we first arrived in India."

"Yes, I've changed. Even my OCD seems better."

In the hot boiling sun, they waited for the bus that would take them to the interior of Punjab as Taj had promised a friend in London that he would visit his elderly parents, who lived in a village there.

Their bus arrived but it would not move until it was full. There were a few seats left.

So desperate was the driver, he was pulling a pedestrian onto the bus.

"Let go of my hand," shouted the pedestrian. "Why are you pulling me?"

"You can travel on half the fare. I will charge you a child's rate."

"No, you idiot. I am walking to my house nearby," screamed the pedestrian.

The people on the bus started to laugh at the driver. He turned on them. "Why you all eating and making a mess?" He pointed to a notice stating that eating on the bus was forbidden.

The man who had just opened his tiffin, full of fried potato parathas and mango pickles, shouted back, "It is our right to eat and drink anywhere. India is a free country."

The driver was called the funny man of Punjab roadways. He was short, obese and middle aged. His black hair was brushed back and glasses perched precariously on his large nose. His khaki uniform looked crumpled and had grease stains on it as if he had been working like a mechanic.

Sandip wanted to go to the toilet.

Taj said, "Go quickly. You don't want to miss this bus."

Sandip asked the ticket office man for directions to the gent's toilet and was told,

"Go straight and turn left at the end."

Sandip walked straight. It was a long walk. He turned left at the end and reached his destination, the farm fields where he emptied his bladder behind the bushes. He ran back but he need not worry, the bus was still there.

More passengers arrived. Only one seat was left now.

The last passenger, an elderly lady, picked her way with a stick, helped by a young man. He told the driver, "My mother is travelling alone. Please tell her when you reach the village Jamira."

"Sure."

"Please don't forget," pleaded the son.

"I will look after her as if she was my own mother. I will not forget," he promised.

The bus started and the passengers clapped. The brothers joined the celebrations.

After driving an hour, the bus did a sudden U-turn.

Everyone was surprised when, twenty minutes later, the bus stopped and the driver told the elderly lady, "You can get down now. It's your village, Jamira."

She thanked him but made no move to get off the bus.

"My son instructed me to take my diabetic medicine when I reached this village because he calculated it as the correct time to take my dose. My own village is your seventh stop from here."

To the great amusement of other passengers, the driver buried his head in his hands.

He muttered, "You stupid woman, I have wasted so much fuel. I forgot to get you down when we reached Jamira so I came back because I felt guilty. If my bus owner finds out, he will not pay my bonus."

The front passenger asked, "Why are you so worried about your bonus?"

"My wife takes all my salary. I need my bonus to sustain my love of alcohol."

He restarted the bus. It began to rain so people closed the windows.

The aroma of fried potatoes, pickles, onions and herbs changed to a pungent smell when someone noisily broke wind.

Sandip quickly opened the window.

The old man sitting in front of the brothers unashamedly said loudly, "Thank God, the gas was troubling me, I feel better now."

Then, there was a loud burp and a voice said, "That's great."

Sandip murmured, "In England, others bless you when you sneeze. Here they bless themselves when they fart or burp!"

They had a good laugh.

Getting wet with rain coming in, Sandip closed the window again.

At the next stop, a vendor boarded, proclaiming, "If you have constipation, wind problems, eye problems and allergies, take one dose of this herbal medicine and you will be cured. Only one rupee a dose."

Sandip said, "It is so bizarre selling medicines on the bus and how can one medicine cure everything?"

Taj replied, "That's cheap. It would help the NHS budget."

Sandip joked, "I think the old man in front needs it more than the NHS!"

The vendor looked at them and said, "You English? I speak English."

The bus started again.

Sandip asked, "Do you think these village men speak English?"

"Oh yes," laughed Taj. "But only at night."

"How come?"

"After drinking alcohol, they start speaking English."

"Really?" asked Sandip.

"But you have to be drunk to understand them!"

The bus reached their destination and they got off in the village square.

They were surprised to see a lady addressing a congregation under the shade of the Banyan tree.

She was saying, "Give the gift of life to baby girls..."

The brothers did not know what she was talking about but Taj insisted they find out more. They waited until she had finished, then approached her and politely introduced themselves.

"I'm Taj and this is my brother Sandip. We are visiting from London and only caught the end of your talk. Is it female empowerment you are talking about?"

She replied, "I am Rani, volunteering for a charity which promotes the education and career promotion of girls."

"But you were addressing mainly older men in the square?" asked Taj.

She laughed and said, "Good question. If you have time, I can give you more information about my charity?"

Sandip was surprised when Taj said they had all the time in the world.

Rani explained, "The ratio of girls in this and the surrounding villages was much less than that of boys. The young wives complained that they had suffered pressure to terminate their pregnancy, if they were found to be having female babies.

"Why?" asked Sandip.

"Because they believed that boys, when they grow up, will work on the farms and look after their parents in old age. The girls, they felt, were a burden on the family. Poor farmers, who had daughters, had to take out loans to give dowry in cash and goods to the bridegroom on the wedding day. This was despite the Indian government making dowry a criminal offence."

Taj asked, "Was your charity successful in its mission?"

"There were so many problems. We researched further and found that mother-in-laws were the main obstacles. They wanted grandsons because they wanted the family tree to continue. They would forcibly send their pregnant daughter-in-laws to the nearby town, where illegal ultrasound clinics determined foetal gender and carried out termination of pregnancy if female."

The brothers were horrified. "That's terrible. Why does the son not support his wife?" asked Sandip, in a voice full of anger.

"The mother-in-law is too powerful. One of the founders of our charity was a scientist. He taught all the charity staff and volunteers about genetic inheritance so they could educate them. After much effort, when the village mother-in-laws understood the scientific explanation, our mission was successful."

Taj asked, "What was this education?"

"The mother-in-laws were told, 'One chromosome is inherited from the mother and one from the father. The male offspring is XY. The female offspring is XX. With a grandson, his Y comes from your son and his X from your daughter-in-law. When you have a granddaughter, her one X comes from your son and the other X from your daughter-in-law. The X from your son is his genetic inheritance from you. So your granddaughter is the only gender which carries your gene.'

"The women were astounded and visibly shaken by this

information. The ratio of girls has increased in all our villages. But to promote education and career opportunities for girls, we had to convince their fathers and grandfathers that it was respectable to do so. Hence me addressing mainly older men in the square today."

Taj was amazed by Rani and her great work. He wanted to stay longer but Sandip insisted they move on.

After thanking Rani, they walked on to the farmhouse where they were met and welcomed by their friend's elderly parents. The farmhouse was grander than they had expected.

The family employed workers on the farm and servants in their house to look after them.

Taj and Sandip enjoyed a meal of fresh farm food, the friend's father assuring them of its hygiene. "This is fresh milk from our cows. Don't worry, it was boiled. Even the drinking water has been boiled and cooled."

After dinner, they were asked, "Do you want to sleep in the room with a ceiling fan or on the rooftop?"

It was a hot summer night. They decided to sleep upstairs.

The servant brought sheets and pillows. There were already beds standing against the wall on the roof. The brothers put them down.

Taj asked the servant, "These are very light beds. Do they stay on the rooftop?"

"Yes, we only bring them down during the monsoon rains," he replied.

Sandip asked, "Are these the ropes between the wooden frame of the bed?"

"No, these are chords, made of jute. When they become loose, I tighten them," he replied. "We call them charpoy beds. Outside, you can see the villagers sitting on them."

They lay under the stars and Sandip said, "It feels like a beautiful surreal blanket above our heads."

Taj was not listening; he was deep in thought.

Taj awoke to the sound of a rooster crowing. There was a fresh wind and it was no longer hot and humid. He went back to sleep for a while and then he shook his brother awake.

"Sandip, get up. Look, the sky is gold," said Taj excitedly.

The birds were chirping

The sun was just peeking out of the horizon, filling the sky with shades of orange and pink.

They were surprised to see green wheat fields all around and a distant river, which seemed like a liquid gold and silver, glistening in the sunrise.

The servant brought a pot of tea with biscuits.

He said, "Bad tea for you."

Taj corrected him, "You mean bed tea?"

He replied, "Yes, yes," with a sleepy smile.

"Thank you very much," said Taj.

They walked round the farm and then followed the path to the river. When they came back, they were served the full Punjabi meal of sarso ka saag with maki di roti and home-made butter with lassi, the yogurt drink.

Sandip asked, "What is this dish?"

The friend's father replied, "It is a traditional Punjabi dish. Sarso ka saag is made from mustard leaves and spices, ginger and garlic. Maki di roti is made from corn flour."

It was quite a heavy meal and Sandip started burping.

"Bless you," said Taj laughing, remembering the bus passengers.

"It is not funny. Unlike Punjabis, I can't eat a heavy meal in the morning."

After breakfast, Taj asked his friend's parents if they knew Rani.

They both spoke highly of her and her charity work.

It was time to go but the brothers had fallen in love with this village. They were touched by the warmth and kindness extended to them by the family.

Taj wondered why his friend, the son of these good people, was working in a factory in London, when he could have a more dignified life in Punjab with his elderly parents on their lovely farm.

They left with a heavy heart and were sad to see the tears in the eyes of the parents when they bade them farewell. They clearly missed their son and longed for the day he would return.

When they approached the village square, they saw Rani at the bus stand. She was tall and straight with long black hair plaited in a thick braid. She wore salwar kameez, bright yellow coloured with a dupatta, a red long scarf, over her shoulders.

Taj walked quickly towards her and said, "Oh, I am so glad, we meet again."

He could not hide his excitement and whispered, "I have been thinking about you."

She smiled shyly. Her face blushed like a flower.

The bus arrived and they boarded together.

Taj sat with Rani and Sandip got into the seat behind them.

Sandip had never seen his brother chatting so passionately with a woman. He saw them exchanging pieces of paper.

When Rani got down, she waved at both of them.

Sandip joined Taj with a grin on his face and said, "So, brother, are you in love?"

৺ 27 ৲

RETURN TO LONDON

One evening before returning to London, Sandip went shopping in Delhi's Connaught place, with its Georgian-style buildings from the British era.

He bought bindi and bangles of different colours for his girl friends in England. For his best friend, he bought a kurta – a long loose garment, like a shirt without a collar, worn commonly in India. For himself, he bought some silk shirts.

Taj's friend had sent his car with the driver to take him shopping. Sandip forgot to take the mobile number of the driver or note the car registration. After shopping, looking for the car, he remembered it was a white Toyota and was relieved to see it. He opened the back door, stashed his shopping bags and sat in the back seat.

He told the driver, "Let's go home."

The driver turned around, looking surprised.

He stared at Sandip and said, "I'm not your driver."

"You are my friend's driver, let's go now."

Sandip heard the driver on his mobile saying, "Madam,

where are you? I am waiting outside the Crazy Camel Ice Cream Parlour."

The voice on the other side echoed in the car. "Wait there, I am on my way."

"But madam, a young man I don't know is sitting in the back seat asking me to take him home."

"No, no, call the police; he must be a car thief."

Sandip quickly got out of the car, apologising to the driver.

He saw a lady running towards the car. He ran away in the opposite direction and managed to catch a taxi to his grandfather's house.

When he told his brother about the incident, Taj laughed and said, "I can imagine you red-faced running with your shopping bags, being chased by a crowd shouting *thief!*"

Next day at Delhi International airport, Taj told Sandip, "Let's have tea, it is known to cool you down on a hot day."

Taj ordered elaichi tea and Sandip hot masala chai.

Sandip asked, "What is elaichi tea?"

"It is cardamom which makes the tea delightfully spicy and gives it a strong aroma. This spice grows in the mountainous parts of India."

After drinking tea, Taj said, "I feel refreshed now, ready for the journey back. I enjoyed the flavour."

It was a long queue at check-in and they were glad to receive their boarding passes.

At the immigration desk, the officer said, "Passport please."

Sandip asked, "Why passport check when I am leaving India?"

Surprised at Sandip's question, the officer's face hardened and his brow furrowed.

He did not reply but took a long time checking their passports. To Taj's relief, he finally stamped the passports. When Taj quickly picked them up, the officer raised an eyebrow.

Walking away Sandip sniggered, "The officer's reaction reminded me of you when I ask a question you don't know the answer to."

Taj glared back, already so tense at the situation.

Sandip joked, "Have elaichi tea, it will cool you down."

Standing in the queue for security, Taj noticed a man with a big belly. He was told to remove his belt before going through the metal detector. While the officer was performing the security pat-down, down came the man's trousers!

Taj quickly looked away embarrassed, promising himself that when he returned to London, he would start eating more healthily.

As their plane took off, Delhi's dazzling lights slowly became distant.

Taj asked Sandip, "Are you sad to leave India?"

"I am returning home but I'll miss India. Beneath the veneer of dust and flies, there is real beauty in this country and of course hospitable people."

"What was your funniest sight in India?"

Sandip replied, "On a wet Delhi day, the sight of man with an open black umbrella, urinating on a back wall of a shop. The funny thing was that he was laughing at the writing on the wall, in black paint in big letters stating, ONLY DONKEYS URINATE HERE."

Taj said, "The shopkeeper must have painted it to shame and stop people urinating?"

Sandip said, "It was strange that there was a public toilet

nearby but people seemed to enjoy urinating in the open and any wall was a target."

Taj said, "Don't you agree that this amazing journey has taught you that there is more to life than party and drinks and materialism?"

"Not really," replied Sandip.

"What do you mean?"

Sandip described his meeting with an Indian holy man and their conversation.

"What is the best way to celebrate life?"

"Celebrate fully, one day before death."

"How do you know when death will strike?"

"No one knows when death will come. So, celebrate every day, for death can arrive the next."

Sandip told Taj, "So, drink, party and be merry every day."

They reached Dubai in time and caught the connecting flight to London. It had been a long day and sleep overwhelmed them.

Taj was woken by the air hostess. "Sir, you ordered a vegetarian meal?"

He had slept for more than five hours. He looked outside his window. Thick clouds everywhere. He told Sandip, "Whenever I see these sun-blocking dense clouds, I know we have entered the European airspace."

The announcement came over. "The weather in London is dull, overcast and cloudy."

"Welcome home," grinned Sandip.

The immigration in London was much quicker than Delhi.

On the way home, Sandip told the Asian taxi driver, "Could I request you to blow your car horn? I miss the constant hooting on Indian roads."

The driver laughed and commented, "In India, they honk to tell other cars, autos, cyclists and pedestrians to move out of the way. The cows walking in the middle of the road are made aware of the overtaking cars. But they overdo it, all the time."

Taj said, "Despite the noise, mother India is our soul, the source of love and contentment."

Sandip said, "India has made my brother spiritual."

He turned to Taj. "Will you now tell your psychology patients to look inwards and meditate?"

"No, I have to follow National Health Service guidelines."

Sandip told Taj, "When you talk of love, it reminds me of Rani."

"I miss her and am going to apply for a visa for her to come here. I'd better tell mum and dad."

"I wish you luck."

The taxi reached their London flat.

"Welcome home," said Sandip. "Fish and chips?"

✵ 28 ✵

ADDICTION

S andip had a friend in his London school, who was expelled, because he was caught selling drugs to other students in the school grounds. His name was Ravi. This is his story.

❦

RAVI WAS BORN AND BROUGHT UP IN LONDON. HE LIVED with his parents. He was an obese 5' 6" carefree man of twenty-six. He would come home late every night, drunk and stoned. He had never worked. He had been spoiled by his mother, since childhood. She gave him money whenever he asked.

If father was ever angry with him, she would protect him, saying, "He is our only child. Don't be harsh with him. Give him love, that will help him."

Dad would tell mum, "Ravi is in the bad company of drug

addicts. We should threaten him that if he does not stop using drugs, he will have to leave our home."

He would shout at Ravi, "Your problem is drugs and alcohol."

"No, they are my solution," he would shout back. "You are always judging me, you always tell me what to do, there is no dialogue."

"Son, please stop taking drugs," pleaded his mother.

Ravi replied, "I get a sense of warmth and contentment with drugs. My mind and body fills with joy."

"Your euphoria is short-lived, my child. If you want contentment, meditate and do yoga."

His father shouted, "Instead of being high on drugs, why don't you become high on work and life?"

When he was a teenager, Ravi was injecting heroin in his groin. Out spurted blood like a fountain. The needle had hit the femoral artery. As fate would have it, he was in the hospital grounds, so luckily he had immediate medical attention. However, he then developed a life-threatening groin infection. His consciousness fluctuated. When he recovered, he was restless, and he wanted drugs again.

When told by the doctor how serious his condition was and that he could not have drugs, he became agitated.

He said, "I saw the world in technicolour. I was flying among layers of colourful patterns. The glorious, multicoloured, layers and layers of them, each one more lovely. It was pure bliss. I felt closer to God."

The doctor said gently, "No, you were not close to God, it was all drug induced."

Fortunately, he recovered from the infection.

His father, Mr Kumar, had come to England from India as a teenager. He worked in factories doing many hours of overtime to earn money, and when he had enough, he opened a corner shop. He worked seven days a week, from dawn to dusk, so he blamed himself for Ravi's drug addiction. "Maybe if I had spent more time with him in his childhood, he would be a better person today."

One day, Ravi was drinking in the pub with Arun, his best friend. Ravi complained that he was having difficulty in getting money from his mother. Drugs were getting expensive.

They had both taken part in house break-ins to obtain the cash, but the last time, it went horribly wrong.

One evening, they saw a pile of unopened milk bottles outside the door of a house and presumed the occupants were away on holiday.

Arun entered through the window while Ravi waited outside, but the occupants were actually inside. Arun panicked and jumped from the first-floor window and suffered a fracture to his ankle as a consequence. The occupants caught him and handed him to the police. Ravi fled the scene.

Today, sitting in the pub, they were talking about that incident.

Ravi said, "I was relieved to reach home safely. Next morning, while I was on the toilet, I heard heavy footsteps on the stairs. Next moment, the police had handcuffed me. How humiliating it was to be caught with your trousers down, sitting on the toilet."

Arun said, "The police handcuffed me and took me to the hospital. I felt lonely and missed your company, so I told the police you were my accomplice."

Ravi shouted, "You bastard, I went to jail for a year because of your confession."

"I also went to jail," said Arun. "Let bygones be bygones. We need to plan for the future. Now, do you want to make money and also have a holiday?"

"No, carrying drugs abroad is a very risky business."

"What I am suggesting is risk free."

"What you mean?" enquired Ravi.

"I know a Sarpanch, a name given to the head of a village council in India. He owns a big farm in Punjab. He has one daughter, aged eighteen. He has no sons. You could demand a big dowry as the condition for marrying his daughter and get rich."

"Sorry, I don't want to get married," said Ravi.

"You then come back to London and she will spend all her life in Punjab, waiting for you."

When they had finished laughing, they booked a flight to India where they got a chauffeur-driven Mercedes from Delhi to Punjab. They arrived at the Sarpanch's house, surrounded by a wheat farm.

Arun introduced Ravi. "He is a businessman from London. He wants to marry your daughter. I am from your neighbouring town."

The Sarpanch was surprised. His daughter, Kiran, was indeed eighteen years old and very good-looking. "You have come all this way to marry my daughter? You must have heard about my daughter's beauty in London?"

As emigrating to London is a dream come true for many Punjabi brides, her father was pleased.

"What do you do in London?" he asked.

"I have factories and hundreds of workers."

"I guessed from your car outside, that you are a rich man."

"Do you mind if he talks to your daughter?" asked Arun.

"Sure, I will call her."

Kiran was five feet two inches tall, slim with a fair complexion. She wore her black hair in a neat ponytail. She had deep dimples when she smiled and they stayed on long after her smile had left her big beautiful eyes.

She had studied in a high school in a nearby town, but she struggled to speak English. Ravi promised her that he would teach her English when she accompanied him to London and she was thrilled.

The Sarpanch said, "It would be my privilege if Ravi marries my daughter."

Ravi touched his feet as a sign of respect. "I promise to look after your daughter all my life."

Arun told him that Ravi could only stay in India for one week, so the marriage date was fixed quickly.

The atmosphere got tense when Arun demanded the dowry of lots of cash and a gold bar before the marriage could take place. The headman was taken aback, so he discussed the matter with his wife.

She said, "Kiran is our only child. Take a loan and pay the dowry for a brighter future for our daughter in London."

The wedding day arrived. Arun helped Ravi to get up on the back of the horse. The white horse was adorned with red and gold rich cloth, pink ribbons and various decorations including red bracelets of bells tied to the front legs.

His rather nervous face was veiled with hanging strings of fresh white flowers and Ravi was sneezing with runny nose. He had red, watering, itchy eyes.

Every time, he sneezed, Arun said, "Bless you."

Ravi shouted, "You stupid man, why did you arrange to cover my face with flowers. You know I'm allergic!"

"It is a local custom."

"Shut up. Quickly take it off my face," shouted Ravi. "Can't you see I'm suffering? All you do is bless me every time I sneeze, you idiot."

Arun took off the headdress of flowers from Ravi's face.

The band started playing. Arun had invited friends from a nearby town. They set off the firecrackers, and the horse bolted. The horse minder fell down. Ravi held the reins tightly. The horse was running wildly in the fields. The friends, the bhangra drummers and the band players were running behind the horse. Even the grazing cows stared at him in amazement, shaking their heads in disbelief. Ravi was thrown off. He landed in the ditch.

Someone shouted, "He needs a donkey. He can't ride a horse."

Arun helped him to get up. His arms and legs were bruised. There was a big hole in the trousers and both knees were bleeding.

Arun apologised. "I'm sorry, my stupid friends frightened the horse by lighting the fireworks right in front of the horse."

Ravi was cursing Arun. "Why did you arrange a wedding horse? A decorated car would have been much better instead."

"I'm sorry, I thought you would enjoy the experience," Arun mumbled meekly.

The Sarpanch came running. He took Ravi to the nearby farmhouse and cleaned his wounds. His relative collected the new suit which had already been stitched for the groom, from his house. Ravi limped to the tractor.

When they approached the bride's house, the friends started dancing to the bhangra beat on the drums. They were so drunk that some of them fell in the gutters by the roadside.

The bridegroom's party reached Kiran's home. Arun went inside the house to get the dowry. He came out smiling and gave the victory sign to Ravi. After the marriage ceremony, Ravi and his friends started binge drinking. There was lots of scotch whisky served.

That night, Kiran in her bridal red lehenga dress, decked in gold jewellery and with her hair tied intricately, waited for Ravi until she fell asleep.

In the early hours, Ravi stumbled on to the decorated bed.

Kiran was woken by Ravi's vomiting. He apologised for excess drinking. She cleaned his face and clothes. It was daytime.

He asked her, "Why did you sleep wearing jewellery? I will take it for safekeeping." She gave him all her jewellery. He also took her gold bangles.

Kiran thought, *What an unromantic wedding night.*

Stony-faced, Arun entered the room

He told Ravi, "Your father suffered a heart attack. He was admitted to hospital in London."

Ravi had told Kiran and his parents-in-law that his dad had not come for the wedding as he had not been well, but the heart attack was a new serious development. He would have to travel to London today.

Kiran asked, "When will I see you?"

"Soon," he replied. "I need to arrange the spouse visa for you to join me in London."

Her eyes welled up with tears. Her mother hugged her. "Don't worry, Ravi will return soon."

Ravi and Arun left quickly.

Ravi told Arun, "You are a good actor. When I saw your serious face, I almost believed my father's heart attack."

They both laughed.

Time passed and there was no phone call from Ravi. Kiran tried to ring him many times every day. After a month, it dawned on the family that they had been deceived. They went to the village police station and filed a complaint against Ravi and Arun.

The officer said, "Don't you know, there are some evil Indian men abroad whose business is to marry and cheat. Didn't you investigate the groom?"

The father said, "I was naive. He wore expensive clothes. He had an expensive car. I said yes to marriage without checking. I thought Arun was from the neighbouring town but we couldn't trace him, either."

The police officer reassured him. "Don't worry, when he enters India again, he will be charged with section 498A of the Indian penal code. It is a non bailable criminal offence for demanding dowry."

"Who will marry my daughter now? It is all my mistake," the father cried.

Kiran lost her sleep, worrying. However, she still believed he would come back. She thought, *If he was an evil man, he would have taken advantage of me. He did not touch me.*

🦚 29 🦚

TAJ BECOMES A CARER

F our months after returning to London, the brothers received the sad news that their grandmother had died. She was their grandfather's carer.

They wanted to bring their grandfather to England but the immigration rules were strict.

The immigration solicitor advised Taj's father, "The parent has to be not only financially dependent but also physically dependent and to prove the latter, they have to stay in India and look after the parent physically for at least six months and then apply for immigration." He warned that if they lost their immigration application to get their father to join them in UK, they would also be refused if they applied for a short-term visitor visa in future.

Taj managed to get six months of unpaid leave and travelled to Delhi as his father, Dr Kohli, a hospital doctor in London, was unable to get leave.

In his grandad's house, the first few weeks as a carer were challenging, despite employing a home help.

One night, Mr Kohli, his grandad, was repeatedly switching lights on and off.

Taj asked, "Why do you do that?"

"I see people peeping into my window."

"Which people?"

"They are short dark people and carry swords."

"Do they say anything?"

"Kill them all, kill them all."

Taj came across a folder in grandma's drawer with a prescription. *Mr Kohli – Diagnosis Alzheimer's.*

Mealtimes were difficult. After finishing his meal, he would say, "Where is my meal?"

"Grandad, you have just eaten."

"You're lying. You want me to die hungry."

Taj decided to leave his grandfather's plate on the table to prove he had eaten, but it led to more shouting.

Taj told grandad, "You are a fast eater. Eat slowly and chew your food. Before eating, smell your food flavours and enjoy your food."

Grandad gave him a blank look.

Taj said, "Look, put your nose above the food and smell the beautiful flavours."

Grandad put his nose close to the plate and quickly lowered it into the rice and vegetable curry.

Taj shouted, "No, no." But it was too late.

He cleaned his grandad's face and decided no more food advice.

Then one morning, his grandad was shouting, "You have stolen my money. You are poisoning me."

Taj was shaken, although he knew that some dementia patients do suffer delusions.

Also, Mr Kohli was becoming incontinent and Taj was struggling to look after his personal care and hygiene. He employed a nurse from an agency to visit his home twice a day. Grandad's behaviour was getting worst. Some days, he was restless and agitated and other days, he didn't want to get out of bed.

One day, Taj sat with him. "Grandad, can you draw me a picture?"

"There are fires everywhere," replied his grandad.

"Fires where?" asked Taj.

No reply.

"Where are you now?" asked Taj again.

"Lahore. Am I safe, are they following me?"

He had sweat on his forehead.

Mr Kohli had been a schoolteacher in a village near Lahore in what is now Pakistan.

Taj realised that dementia had taken him to 1947 when Mr Kohli had fled from newborn Pakistan and had seen killings on both sides of the border in Punjab.

Taj decided to learn about his grandfather's journey during the 1947 partition from his great uncle.

His great uncle told him, "Your grandfather had never talked of painful memories but since a year ago, he has been talking of those terrible events and repeating them again and again. We were two of the ten million people who became refugees when the British divided India and created a Muslim-majority Pakistan. Hindus and Sikhs headed East to Indian Punjab and Muslims went west. We saw horrendous communal violence and lost our parents in this hatred. It was shocking because Hindus, Sikhs and Muslims had lived peacefully for hundreds of years. I blame the outsiders; our village Muslims protected and helped us to escape."

Taj thought of his visit to the Wagah border where millions of refugees crossed in opposite direction.

One day, Taj pointed at the photograph of his late grandmother on the wall and asked his grandfather, "Whose photo is that?"

"I don't know."

"She is your wife."

"No, my wife is Shanti."

Shanti was a domestic help. She was a bubbly young girl of nineteen. Her mother was a servant in their household. Mr Kohli had helped in her education by encouraging her mother to send her to school and supporting the family financially. She called him Papaji and respected him like her own father.

She would say, "Papaji sit down, let me read you today's Hindi newspaper, there are some amusing stories."

She would then laugh with him, "I have seen you dancing to Bhangra music with your walking stick in one hand and a glass of whisky in the other."

She liked wearing colourful saris with matching bindis on her forehead. She enjoyed seeing Bollywood movies on the laptop Taj had gifted her on his last visit.

Taj was relieved Shanti hadn't heard the conversation. He mentioned it to the psychiatrist.

The psychiatrist explained, "Your grandad's memory has gone back in time. In his mind, he is now a young man. When he looked at your late grandmother's photo, he saw an old lady who couldn't be his wife. Shanti is more of his age and caring, so in his mind, she is his wife."

While cleaning the house, Shanti put on the radio.

Hearing clapping from grandad's room, Taj peeped in. Grandad's face was full of smiles. With his arms raised above his shoulders, he was clapping and moving his shoulders up and down. The radio was playing an old Bollywood song.

Taj realised that the song had brought back memories of his youth.

When grandad tried to get up from the bed, he rushed in to help him.

Without his walking stick, he wanted to dance.

Taj thought, even dementia is no bar to the power of music.

⚜

THE NEXT MORNING, TAJ WAS IN THE BATH WHEN SHANTI banged on the door

"Sir, Mr Kohli is missing. He was sitting at the breakfast table and I was in the kitchen, but when I came back he was gone."

Taj quickly came out to the street outside.

"Shanti, I will run in this direction and you run in the opposite direction."

There were no sightings of Mr Kohli.

Taj felt helpless. All kinds of terrible thoughts flooded in:

He may have fallen under a car. He is not wearing warm clothes, the cold December will kill him.

Then suddenly he saw Shanti holding his grandad's hand.

His heart jumped with joy and he hugged his grandad like never before.

He told Shanti, "Well done. Where did you find him?"

"I heard dogs barking in the side street and there was Mr Kohli shouting obscenities.

"'You son of a bitch, I will kill you,' he was screaming."

Taj decided from now on, the door would be locked at all times.

He slept in his grandad's bedroom and one night he awoke and it was daylight. He was surprised, as he had not been disturbed nor taken grandad to the toilet at night. He removed the blanket to wake him up but grandad was lying still. He was breathing heavily and not moving. Taj was worried and telephoned the doctor who came quickly as he lived in a flat in the same building. He called the ambulance and Mr Kohli was admitted to a private hospital. The doctors checked him, did blood tests and an ECG. They told Taj, "He has suffered a stroke and his kidneys are not working well. Blood tests show that he is severely anaemic and needs blood."

"Sure, please go ahead with blood transfusion."

"No, you need to give blood before your grandfather receives the transfusion."

Taj said, "I appreciate that, I am a blood donor in UK."

The doctor replied, "We rely on a family replacement system. If you need blood, you have to find a relative or friend to give it and then we get the appropriate blood from the blood bank."

Taj agreed and gave blood. His grandad was started on the blood transfusion.

Taj's father caught the first flight to Delhi.

Taj and his dad decided that Mr Kohli should only have tender loving care.

The consultant physician ordered brain scans and started grandad on anti-parkinsonian drugs.

"Why don't the consultants here listen to the wishes of the close relatives," Dr Kohli grumbled. "I specifically told them not to order investigations or start drugs which are not urgently required."

The next day when Taj and his dad arrived at the hospital, they were told, "Mr Kohli has been transferred to the intensive care unit because he was breathless."

Dr Kohli noticed that his dad was not breathless now and his observations were stable. He talked to the consultant cardiologist in the ICU who agreed that Mr Kohli could be transferred to the general ward, but the consultant physician in charge refused.

Mr Kohli told the physician, "The only reason for keeping him in the ICU is to make money."

"You are an Indian doctor but you work abroad and then come back big-headed and interfere with our medical management!"

"You are continuing treatment unnecessarily and the only reason is profit, not patient care," said Dr Kohli.

"I'm sorry you question my medical ethics. You have insulted me and I am discharging your father from my care immediately."

Dr Kohli approached the private hospital management. The cardiologist agreed to take over his father's care but the rule was that all the dues had to be paid to the hospital before a different consultant can intervene. The bill was quite high and it took half a day to arrange the payment. Mr Kohli was in a hospital bed but not registered as a patient. Hence, no care from the doctors or nurses was provided until the full payment was received by the hospital.

"Son, we should always be grateful for our national health

service in the UK which looks after us from the cradle to the grave," said Dr Kohli to Taj.

"Dad, I have never seen you so confrontational as you were with that consultant."

"I think I over-reacted," said Dr Kohli sheepishly.

Taj then overheard a conversation between the consultant and a patient's son

"Your mother's case is hopeless with no chance of recovery."

"I will take my mother home for a peaceful death rather than see her dying with machines in a hospital."

"She is your mother and she deserves all the treatments we can give to keep her alive."

"I am already in debt but I will take a loan," said the son, with tears in his eyes.

The cardiologist in charge for Mr Kohli was a doctor with empathy. He advised that loving care can be given at home with support from the hospital. The plan was to discharge him after meeting with the multidisciplinary team to organise home care.

But the next day, Mr Kohli became drowsy and developed a chest infection and never returned home.

Dr Kohli was devastated. Guilty feelings flooded in.

"He encouraged and supported me to become a doctor but I served everyone except him. I served the people of Britain but when it was my turn to look after my old father, the politicians made the immigration rules so strict," sobbed Dr Kohli.

He said angrily, "I know of many NHS doctors whose application for entry to the UK for their elderly parents has been refused. It is so unfair."

Tears welled up in Taj's eyes. As his grandad's carer, he had become even closer to him.

Sandip also arrived from London to attend his grandad's funeral cremation ceremony.

Draped in white cloth, atop a massive pile of wood, lay the body. With the fire and the chanting of prayers, the ceremony had started.

"The soul gets engulfed in the flames and releases from the body," said the mourner standing next to Sandip.

Sandip had never seen a traditional funeral pyre.

Sandip held Taj's hand and said, "I can't stand to see grandad on the pyre with flames. I am feeling dizzy and sweaty."

Taj led him outside and gave him a glass of water.

Tears started to stream down his face.

Together, the brothers wept and hugged.

❧ 30 ❧

SURVIVAL

Taj and Sandip visited their great uncle, Joginder Singh, to learn more about their late grandfather, Vinod Kohli.

Joginder was a Sikh and Vinod, a Hindu.

He was a tall, well dressed elderly man wearing a red turban, a red tie and a matching handkerchief in his coat pocket. His uncut white beard was smartly set. Taj noticed that his smile, his gait and even the way he sat on the settee, reminded him of his grandfather. He loved playing golf every morning in a posh Delhi club, which had opened during the British rule. He also enjoyed drinking whisky with his friends. He said, "Golf, whisky and friends are keeping me young."

"How was it, that you two brothers had different religions?" asked Taj.

"Our parents were Hindus but they wanted to make their eldest son a Sikh."

"How come?"

"I don't know. I remember my father telling me that he felt

blessed when he first took me to a Gurdwara – a Sikh place of worship. I think, in our village in West Punjab, there was a tradition among some Hindu families of making their first-born son a Sikh."

"What happened to the family in August, 1947?" asked Taj.

"Dad had a big farm and lots of workers to till the land. We were a loving family and I remember my happy childhood days. I never thought our good life would come to such an abrupt end."

"Why, what happened then?"

"Vinod and me were sleeping, when dad woke us up and rushed us outside, through the rear door into the fields. He was screaming *stay here, I'll get mum*. He went back into the house and we never saw him again. We saw our house burning and heard the deafening chants of, *kill them! kill them all!*"

He continued with a choking voice, "We hid in the fields. I wanted to go inside the house and check for mum and dad but Vinod wouldn't let me. He cried all night. Whenever I heard sounds, I would cover his mouth, in case his crying attracted the attention of mobs. We kept awake all night and early morning, saw an army convoy. We ran towards them.

"They checked our house and told me that both parents were dead and we had to move on to India. We had no time to grieve.

"I saw burning houses on both sides of the border. The British partition of India had uprooted millions of people and caused intense suffering on both sides of the border."

Joginder covered his face and sobbed, "I have felt guilty all my life. The soldiers did not allow me to see my parents but I should have insisted and given them a religious cremation in the fields, where my father spent all his life, tilling the land. I should have given them a dignified farewell."

Taj hugged his great uncle. He got him a glass of water. Joginder told him not to worry and that he wanted to continue with his story.

"How old were you?"

"I was 16 years old and your grandfather was only 12 years old. He was so frightened, he would not let go of my hands even when sleeping, for many months after coming to India."

"You were housed in a refugee camp in Delhi?"

"Yes, for about six months, then a friend told us that there was a house in Paharganj, old Delhi, whose occupants had fled to Pakistan and we could occupy that house.

"We went at night. It was quiet and all the neighbours seemed to be sleeping. We started breaking the locks. Then suddenly a commotion; it was the end of the midnight show in the cinema opposite the house. People emerged singing Bollywood songs. We lay low until the crowds disappeared."

Taj asked, "Is it not illegal to break locks?"

"It was quite common then and the police turned a blind eye."

"How was your life in India then?" asked Taj.

"It was tough. We sold hair ribbons at Delhi railway station. We had to bribe the railway police to sell on the platforms. Then, there were gangs who carried knives and if you sold on their so-called territory, you could be stabbed. Once we were chased by the gangs. Vinod was pushed down onto the railway tracks. A train was approaching. I jumped from the platform and grabbed my brother's hand and pulled him from the path of the oncoming train. It was a narrow escape.

"Vinod was bruised and shaken. He said, 'I want to go back to my village. We were happy there. We had a big house. We played in the fields, lush green with water everywhere. Here, we live in crowded tents and fight for water every day. There is no school, we struggle to earn few rupees. Mum gave me everything I needed.'"

Joginder said, "I started looking for jobs but soon realised it was a huge problem to find jobs for refugees. We became hawkers, selling old clothes in the streets.

"We made enough money to get a permanent stall in the market. We sold all kinds of clothing and jewellery. Once, we bought clothes labelled – Made by USA. The clothes were stitched by a tailor named Udham Singh Arora. He put the initials of his name on the label. Your grandfather, a teenager then, was shouting outside the stall, come in and buy American shirts for only one rupee. He was proud to be successful in getting so many people to buy his USA clothes!"

Taj smiled. "I have always seen grandad as a wealthy man."

"We worked hard for 15 years on a stall. I and your late grandad then became entrepreneurs and were successful in making plastic buckets. Then we lost money as we made beautifully flavoured toothpaste but it would not come out from the nozzle of the plastic tube! We used it by cutting the tube and distributed it free to the neighbourhood. We employed technicians and were successful in manufacturing adhesives and then car paints. Our factory employed more than 300 workers!"

"What an amazing story after the trauma of 1947," murmured Taj.

"I suffered another traumatic event in my own country on the 31st October 1984.

"I landed at Delhi airport on that day. I visited the toilet and overheard a conversation between the cleaners. 'All Sikhs in Delhi have been killed, none are now left alive.'

"I thought I must have heard wrong.

"I went to the taxi stand and the taxi driver said, 'It is very risky for Sikhs.'

"'Why?' I asked.

"'Don't you know?' A Sikh has shot the prime minister, there are anti-Sikh riots and burnings and killings,' said the taxi driver.

"I thought he was exaggerating. Sikhs have always given their lives for India. Sikh gurus sacrificed their lives protecting Hinduism. Anti-Sikh riots could not be true.

"'I'll pay you double fare, let's go,' I told the taxi driver.

"'I'll take you but if the mob comes, I'll drop you and race away. I don't want to get killed. They will burn my taxi.'

"On the way, I saw burning shops and vehicles. Wherever there were mobs, I put my head down. I was trembling with fear and relieved to reach home and see Hindus and Sikhs together, guarding their streets.

"Your grandfather cried over the senseless killings of innocent Sikh families and said, 'How could you divide us, we are the roots of the same tree, we need to water the tree and make it stronger.'

"'Whenever I think of 1984, a shiver runs down my spine although more than three decades have elapsed," said Joginder.

❧ 31 ❧

BLIND LOVE

It had been a week since grandad's funeral.

Dr Kohli told Taj and Sandip that they should return to London. But he and their mum would stay behind to settle the property and other affairs in Delhi.

Taj said, "I took six months leave to look after grandad but he left us in two months. Could I stay a bit longer?"

"Why are your hands shaking?" asked his dad.

"I have to tell you both something important."

"Go on."

"I should have told you in London but with the sudden death of grandma and my return to India, I could not. On my last visit to India, I met Rani."

"Who's Rani?" asked Dr Kohli.

"Sandip and I met her in a village doing charity work..."

"You're not answering my question."

Taj's mum told dad to give him time and there was no need to rush him.

Taj started again. "Rani is intelligent and good looking. I like her very much. I want to marry her."

"So, it is blind love with a village girl. But what's the rush to marry?"

Seeing the tears in Taj's eyes, his mum hugged him and said, "Don't worry, we'll meet Rani and her parents."

"Marriage is one of life's biggest decisions. Should they not get to know each other before getting married?" said Dr Kohli.

Mrs Kohli snorted. "Did we spend time getting to know each other before marriage?"

"Our families were from similar backgrounds; we were both doctors," replied Dr Kohli.

"Our parents decided our marriage. Did we have any option?" asked Mrs Kohli.

"But you love me, don't you?"

"Of course I do," replied Mrs Kohli.

Mrs Kohli asked Taj to arrange a visit with Rani's family.

Back in their bedroom, Sandip told Taj that the tears of love in his eyes caused an argument of love and marriage between their mum and dad.

"In our parents' generation, what came first, love or marriage?" asked Sandip.

"Marriage of course," replied Taj.

"But what came first, chicken or egg?"

"Depends on what you ordered!" replied Taj, laughing.

Next day, Rani's parents welcomed Taj, Sandip, Mr and Mrs Kohli in their two-bedroom house with a big garden in front.

Rani's dad was a headmaster of the village primary school. Her mum was a housewife.

After lunch, Dr Kohli said, "My son, Taj, is interested in marrying Rani. What do you and Rani think of the proposal?"

"Rani, me and my wife are pleased. However, I do have some anxiety as a girl from our village, Kiran, got married to Ravi from London last year. He took all the dowry, cash and jewellery and never returned back, leaving Kiran in India."

Sandip looked at Taj who was open-mouthed, wide-eyed, staring without blinking. Sandip asked in a soft shaky voice, "Sorry to hear that, how is she?"

Rani's father replied that she still believes that he will come back but her parents are suffering with guilt and depression, having lost all hope of seeing their so-called son in law.

Taj reassured him that he would look after Rani all his life. He then asked Rani if she would show him around the village.

She quickly led him out.

He asked her, "Did you know this girl, Kiran?"

"Yes, we went to same schools, both primary and secondary."

"I am sorry to tell you that Sandip knew Ravi from his school days in London. But let's talk about ourselves."

He told Rani about himself, his family and his job.

Rani said that this village is where she was born and brought up with happy childhood memories.

She attended her father's primary school, than a secondary school in the nearby town.

Having graduated with bachelor of arts in English from a college in the same town, she became a teacher in the village primary school.

'Your graduation in English has made you a good speaker," interrupted Taj.

"I started volunteering for the charity. You already know about that. My passion is education of village girls," continued Rani.

Walking by the side of the river, it was calm and peaceful.

Taj said, "I am looking forward to spending my life with you. But are you happy to marry me?"

"Yes, of course," replied Rani.

Her mobile rang.

It was her father asking them to come back.

When they reached home, he said, "Sorry to call you back but we needed you to decide the wedding date." The big day was fixed for the Sunday in four weeks' time.

On the way home, Mrs Kohli said, "Rani is not only good looking but also a good cook. Her lunch dishes were so delicious."

Sandip said, "Taj's belly will look round like a chapati after marriage."

Ignoring the comment, Taj told his parents that he wanted a simple marriage and no dowry.

He was worried about Rani's family having to take a loan to meet the wedding expenses.

His mother agreed with Taj that they should share the expenses equally.

When Rani's father was told about Taj's request, he said that in India the bride's parents are responsible for all the wedding expenses but when Dr Kohli insisted on sharing, he agreed.

On the wedding day, Rani's house and the garden trees in front were decorated with lights.

Sandip said, "It reminds me of Christmas lights back home."

After the simple marriage ceremony, Taj couldn't find his shoes.

Sandip noticed some girls giggling at Taj.

He asked them, "Why are you giggling?"

"We have hidden your brother's shoes."

"What nonsense," grumbled Sandip.

Taj calmed him down and told him that hiding shoes was an Indian wedding tradition.

The bride's sisters and close friends gave back shoes only when the groom paid them money.

Sandip said, "Had I known, I would have protected them or brought a spare pair of shoes."

"Don't be a kill-joy, look at the happy faces of these girls," replied Taj.

The girls told Taj, "You are British so you pay us £100.00 to get your shoes back."

"That's theft," Sandip shouted.

Taj quickly paid them Rs 10,000 – roughly equal to what the girls had demanded.

Watching them, Mrs Kohli said, "The girls will share the money equally but the real fun is haggling between the groom and the girls when the groom is called a miser and other similar names when he doesn't pay what the girls are demanding."

Today, the girls were clapping and calling Taj, 'A true English gentleman'.

One of these girls approached the brothers.

She said, "I am Kiran. My husband also lives in London. After our marriage, he got busy there but he will surely come back to take me with him."

"I'm sure he will," said Sandip.

Feeling sorry for her, he decided he would meet Ravi on his return.

Now it was time for the photographs of the married couple with the guests.

Standing in the queue were the many invited villagers with boxes of gifts in their hands.

Among them was an engineer on holiday from the USA.

Describing Rani's father, he said, "He taught generations of children to believe in themselves, to work hard and that there was nothing they could not accomplish. I was lucky to be his student in the village primary school."

During photos, the tradition of guests putting sweets in the mouth of the couple brought much laughter.

Every time the photographer said, 'Smile please,' the guest would put barfi or gulab jamun in Taj's mouth. His face looked funny with puffy cheeks.

Being a British gentleman, he didn't even tell the guests to break the sweets into smaller pieces before giving them to him. He tolerated all with a smile.

When someone put the big ball of laddoo in his mouth, not only were his cheeks puffed but his eyes now looked squinted. But smile he did! as the photographer clicked.

"Poor Taj," said his mother. "He will suffer with diarrhoea with eating so much sweet mathai."

After applying for a spouse visa for Rani, Taj returned to London, promising her that she would join him soon.

BACK IN LONDON, SANDIP VISITED HIS OLD SCHOOL FRIEND, Ravi.

He was surprised to see him working in his dad's shop.

"You run your dad's shop?" asked Sandip.

"Yes."

"What a change in you."

"My trip to India has completely changed me."

"How come?"

"When I returned to London, my mother was dying in the hospital. Just imagine, the day I was cheating the innocent bride and her family, on that very day, my mother suffered a massive heart attack. God punished me by taking away from me the person I loved the most. I decided no life of crime, only hard work and charity. I have completely stopped taking drugs."

"I am sorry to hear about your mother," said Sandip. "How are you coping?"

"I have sleepless nights. I think of Kiran and feel guilty and ashamed."

"Would you like to apologise to Kiran?"

"Yes, but would she accept my apologies? How could she accept me as her husband after my hideous behaviour?"

"She is waiting for you to come back," said Sandip, going on to tell him about how he met Kiran in the village.

Tears welled up in Ravi's eyes. He said, "I'll travel to India and bring her back to London."

When Sandip told his brother about Ravi going to India, Taj was worried that Ravi would be arrested on entering India as he was aware of a dowry police case against him.

He rang Rani regarding Ravi coming back and told her that Ravi was now a genuinely reformed person.

She talked to her father, who approached Kiran's dad and convinced him to withdraw the police complaint.

In London, Ravi wept and told his dad about his religious marriage and cheating in India.

Dad told him that wedding pheras are a promise not only to your spouse but also to God that you will be faithful to each other for the rest of your lives. He encouraged him to visit Kiran.

Ravi said, "I feel as if a big weight has been lifted off my shoulders."

On landing in Delhi, he took a taxi to Punjab.

When approaching the village, he saw the fields where he fell in the ditch after the wedding horse bolted. But he was more worried about how he would be treated at his in-laws' house. Finally, his taxi arrived at Kiran's house. Shaking with fear, he knocked.

Kiran opened the door and hugged him. Tears started running down her cheeks.

She mumbled meekly, "I always trusted you to come back."

A tsunami of relief engulfed him. He burst into tears and said, "Forgive me. I will respect you for the rest of my life."

Kiran's father welcomed him to the house. Ravi begged for forgiveness and gave all the dowry cash, gold bars and jewellery back to him.

He was treated well in the village. His mother-in-law said, "All's well that ends well. We thank Taj, Rani and Sandip for helping us to get together."

After a few days, Ravi and Kiran visited the British high commission in Delhi to apply for an entry visa.

Thanks to a helpful official, Kiran got her visa rather quickly.

The day came for Ravi and Kiran to leave the village for London.

Villagers gathered outside the house. The man with the dhol drum was beating on both sides with his stick. As the bhangra rhythm on the drum started, men and women raised their arms above the shoulders and started dancing.

Their taxi left with children running and waving behind them.

People working in the fields also waved at them.

Ravi thought, *what a loving community.*

Kiran said, "We are starting our lives together. We will lean on each other's strengths and forgive each other's weaknesses."

Rani was envious that Kiran had left for UK but she was still waiting.

Eventually, her spouse visa arrived.

Waiting at Heathrow airport in the cold month of December, Taj was excited to see Rani.

Driving home, he drove through the high street to show her the Christmas decorations.

When he approached his residential area, she said, "It reminds me of Diwali in India. The houses have beautiful light decorations."

One January morning, it was snowing. Taj came outside and something hit him on the head.

On opening his eyes, he saw Rani laughing with her hands full of snow. He picked up the snow from the ground and chased her.

After the snowball fight, she said, "That was really fun."

Taj was glad that Rani was feeling at home in London.

She started applying for jobs and managed to get a job in the customer services department of a large company.

Life moved fast. Just before their first marriage anniversary, Rani became pregnant.

They celebrated by asking a few friends to dinner. Among them were Kiran and Ravi.

Kiran still missed her carefree village life. She worked hard with Ravi in their newsagent shop.

Her father-in-law had stopped working due to health reasons.

She said, "I am lucky, Ravi helps me in the kitchen and also cleaning the house."

Rani's pregnancy was uneventful and they were thrilled to have baby boy.

Dr and Mrs Kohli celebrated with a big party in the hotel.

Life was good.

❄ 32 ❄

A FINAL TWIST

One day, Taj was looking for his old photo album in the cupboard. At the back, he noticed an envelope with his name and address.

Opening it, he read, "This to inform you that as advised by you, the deed title of your property...has been transferred from Mr Taj Kohli to Mrs Rani Kohli.

With racing thoughts, a pounding heartbeat, he felt dizzy and sat down.

Rani had not returned from work.

With shaking hands, he telephoned Sandip.

On being told about the letter, Sandip said, "This is fraud."

"But why would Rani do it? She is happy with me. We have a lovely child."

Sandip advised him not to tell Rani about the letter but to investigate.

He asked, "Where is the letter from? When is it dated?"

"It is from a local solicitor's office and dated only one week ago," replied Taj.

Next morning, Taj visited the office. The solicitor recognised him.

He said, "Your application to transfer the title of deeds from your name to your wife's name has been completed."

"But I don't remember applying for..."

"You came to my office. Your wife filled the form and both of you signed in front of me," said the solicitor. He got up and showed him the form for transfer of whole of registered title, which was signed by Taj and Rani.

He asked Taj, "Is this your signature?"

Taj looked at it and nodded. Embarrassed, he walked out of the office.

Back at his flat, when he parked his car, he did not remember driving from the solicitor's office.

He started questioning his sanity.

At home, Sandip was waiting for him.

After hearing the conversation with the solicitor, he advised Taj to involve the police.

"No, never," replied Taj. "I love Rani. If she had asked me to transfer my flat to her name, I would have willingly..."

He was interrupted by his mobile ringing. It was the solicitor.

"Thinking back to the day you came to my office, you didn't look well. Every time I asked you a question, your wife replied. She said that you were suffering with a severe migraine. Do you want me to take any action?"

"No, it's fine. Leave it with me," replied Taj.

He had never suffered headaches.

That night, he could not sleep. He heard the baby crying. Rani got up and went over to the baby's room.

Looking across the bed, there was Rani's mobile with the screen lit up.

Glancing at it revealed messages flashing from Tommy the Tarzan.

He was going to get up to get his glasses when he heard Rani's footsteps coming back.

Quickly lying down, he pretended to be asleep.

Next day, he told Sandip about the mobile messages.

Sandip visited Kiran and asked her if she knew Tommy the Tarzan.

She replied that there was a boy by that name in the high school in Punjab she and Rani attended.

Sandip asked, "Were he and Rani friends?"

"I don't know. He was always trying to impress her."

"What did he look like?"

"He was dark skinned, brawny and heavily built. A bodybuilding contest winner, he was popular with girls, who loved his big muscles."

Sandip informed Taj about what Kiran had told him about Tommy the Tarzan and begged him to get the police involved. But Taj refused and was not happy that Sandip had involved Kiran. "What about Rani's reputation?" he asked.

Wanting to help his brother, Sandip told mum and dad Taj's problems.

Dr Kohli was furious. "With her captivating smile and her sweet talk, Rani has charmed our son. He adores her so much that he cannot see how she is cheating him."

Mrs Kohli warned her husband not to get angry with Taj. "It is an infatuation. But patience and love will help him to see through his obsession with her."

Dr Kohli decided to seek help from a private-detective agency in London, run by an Indian.

He said, "We specialise in cases of cheating spouses. I have contacts in India so they could do surveillance of Tommy the Tarzan there."

Next day, the detective started following Rani.

Outside her office, he photographed her talking to a man.

When she left in the evening, the same man was waiting again. She accompanied him to a cafe.

With the photograph in his hands, Sandip visited Kiran.

"It is him, Tommy the Tarzan. What's he doing in London?" asked Kiran, surprised. "How come you have his photo?"

Ignoring her question, Sandip quickly left, convinced that Rani and Tommy were planning to sell Taj's flat and elope together.

The private investigator started following Tommy also.

He reported that Tommy was staying with three other men in a rundown house in West London.

While following him one day, he saw Tommy acting suspiciously and in a side street, he was selling white packets.

The next day, while following Tommy, he entered a shopping centre.

In the public toilets, he was in the cubicle adjacent to the one used by Tommy.

The detective had his recording device ready to listen to any conversation from the next cubicle.

Hearing a sound of something falling on the floor, he knelt down and looked under the cubicle partition.

Lying on the floor was a handgun.

Quickly coming out, he telephoned the police.

There was a commotion. Running into the toilet area were officers with guns.

The investigator pointed to the closed cubicle.

"Police, come out with your hands in the air."

"I can't. I am suffering with diarrhoea."

The officers kicked the door open.

Sitting on the toilet was Tommy, trembling with his trousers down.

Quickly he was handcuffed. The officer picked up the gun from the floor.

"You do not have to say anything but it may harm your defence if you do not mention when questioned something you later rely on in court. Anything you do say may be given in evidence."

The officer pulled Tommy's trousers up and led him out of the cubicle.

"I have a right to clean myself," said Tommy.

"Only after you have been strip searched in the police station," replied the officer.

With handcuffs behind his back, watched by crowds of shoppers, he was taken away.

In the police cell, the officer asked Tommy, "Give me your mobile password."

"No."

"You cannot refuse as you are being investigated for terrorist action."

Frightened, Tommy opened his mobile.

Looking at the texts, the officer was surprised.

There were hundreds of messages to Rani which started only three months ago.

The first one read, "I have found out that you are now

married and living in London. I want you to transfer Rs10,000 to me, otherwise I will publish your private photos."

Rani replied, "You were my boyfriend for only a short time but you spiked my drink and took photos against my will. I wish I had reported you to the police in India. I hate you but knowing how evil you are, I will send you money provided you destroy all my private material, you illegally possess."

More messages asking Rani for more and more money.

Finally, Rani seemed to have had enough.

She messaged, "To hell with you. I am not sending you any more money. You can do whatever you want."

Then a break and again a message from Tommy to Rani. "I am in London. I need £100,000. I know your address. If you don't pay, your husband will come to harm."

"Please don't harm him. I love him more than myself. But who has so much money?"

"You can sell your flat."

"It is my husband's, not mine."

"You can transfer the flat to your name."

"You are not only a repulsive and revolting person but also insane."

"No, I am serious. I can provide you with a white powder which you put in his drink. It will temporarily affect his memory and you can get him to sign the legal papers. If you don't comply, your husband will suffer. But if you sell and pay me, I promise never to bother you again," messaged Tommy.

After interrogation, the police did not find evidence of terrorism or drug dealing. But he was charged with illegal possession of a firearm.

The officer also contacted Rani. She became a police

witness in the court and Tommy was also charged with blackmailing.

The court hearings were difficult but she was relieved when Tommy was sent to jail for fifteen years and to be deported to India after the prison sentence.

Embracing her in the courtroom, Taj said, "Rani, I always believed in you."

Dr Kohli also hugged her. "Taj's love for you was not blind. It was a true love."

With tears in her eyes, Mrs Kohli said, "My heart goes out to you. It is hard to imagine how much suffering you have been through."

"I'm really sorry for doubting you," said Sandip.

Rani wept. "I want to forget the bad days and look forward to happy days with Taj and my baby. I hope life is now full of joy, love and positivity."

Sandip went over to Taj. He said, "We went together to explore the spirit of India. But neither of us imagined it would end in a London courtroom."

With tears in their eyes, they hugged each other.

ABOUT THE AUTHOR

My name is Surinder Singh Jolly, and I am a retired medical doctor. I was born and raised in Kenya, moving to India in my teens and remaining there to study Medicine. A few years after I graduated, I moved to the UK in 1979, with my wife, also a doctor, to continue practising here. Since then, I have worked in various NHS hospitals across the UK and ultimately settled as a General Practitioner in Manchester, where we have raised our 3 daughters.

In 2009, I was awarded an MBE by the Queen, for services to medicine and healthcare.

My inspiration for this book came from my personal experiences, my love for India, and my reflections on East meets West.

If you enjoyed this book, please help to spread the word by leaving a review on Amazon, Goodreads or any other suitable forum. These are a huge help to authors.

COMING SOON

*A **Collection of Peacock Feathers*** contains short stories based in India, providing a bird's eye view into a different culture.

In India is a gold mine of amazing experiences.

This collection provides a unique insight into the joys, sorrows, challenges, sights and sounds, customs and rituals of India.

The stories are memorable, varied and entertaining, making you cry with laughter and frustration in turn at the hilarious tragedy of human affairs.

Within these pages, you will experience a rollercoaster of emotions.

It truly is a journey of discovery.

ACKNOWLEDGEMENTS

Thank you to my wife, Gursharan. Her invaluable support made this book possible.

Thanks to my daughters, Jasleen, Ishveen and Kavneet, for all their encouragement.

After my NHS retirement, I completed a course in creative writing. The tutor, Carmen Walton, inspired me to write with confidence.

More than two years ago, I joined a writers' group led by Jill Quigley. It became a family, a supportive environment to enjoy writing where members gave invaluable advice. Thank you to all.